She did not   ***d***
for it...

Jeb's mouth was on hers, delicious as salted caramel. Haley knew that this was an experience she would never forget: the sound of the billowy sails flapping in the Atlantic breeze; the July sun beaming down bright and hot, shining a million tiny fractured lanterns over the choppy caps of blue water; the smell of briny ocean spray; this handsome man, hard with muscles and a gorgeous smile, kissing a practical woman who'd forgotten what it was like to have fun.

She should break off the kiss. She knew it. *Do something!* Anything! Just stop kissing him!

But she did none of those things.

Instead, she twined her arms around his neck and pulled him down on top of her.

Harley couldn't think straight. Acting like this was so unlike her. She felt as if she were channeling some spritely mermaid turning the tables on a handsome fisherman by catching him in her net. Oddly thrilling, that image.

You are in such trouble, whispered her brain....

Dear Reader,

One of the fun things about being a writer is the research. On the surface, research might sound boring. Dry and dusty. Hours spent poring over books. Except, that's not the kind of research I'm talking about. For *Smooth Sailing,* my research entailed going to a marina and asking to be taken out on a sailboat. It meant taking a class in sailing and spending hours talking to avid sailors. Now that's just downright fun.

I learned boating safety, the difference between the sails, the names of all the ropes, the way to properly launch a sailboat, how to trim the sail, how to throw a line, tie up the boat, how to recover from a capsize and how not to panic if you fall overboard. What I took away from this experience is that sailing is really complicated and I have a whole new respect for the sport and the people who sail.

What I hope is that my dedication to research paid off and you'll be able to experience sailing right along with the hero and heroine of *Smooth Sailing,* Jeb Whitcomb and Haley French, who fall in love on the high seas. It's a grand adventure and I thank you for taking the ride with me.

Smooth Sailing is the second book in the Stop the Wedding! series. I hope you'll be on the lookout next month for the final installment in the trilogy, *Crash Landing.* Until next time...

Happy reading,

Lori Wilde

Smooth Sailing

Lori Wilde

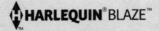

HARLEQUIN® BLAZE™

Recycling programs
for this product may
not exist in your area.

ISBN-13: 978-0-373-79746-2

SMOOTH SAILING

Copyright © 2013 by Laurie Vanzura

This edition published by arrangement with Harlequin Books S.A.

For questions and comments about the quality of this book,
please contact us at CustomerService@Harlequin.com.

® and TM are trademarks of Harlequin Enterprises Limited or its
corporate affiliates. Trademarks indicated with ® are registered in the
United States Patent and Trademark Office, the Canadian Trade Marks
Office and in other countries.

Printed in U.S.A.

www.Harlequin.com

ABOUT THE AUTHOR

Lori Wilde is a *New York Times* bestselling author and has written more than forty books. She's been nominated for a RITA® Award and four *RT Book Reviews* Reviewers' Choice Awards. Her books have been excerpted in *Cosmopolitan*, *Redbook* and *Quick & Simple*. Lori teaches writing online through Ed2go. She's also an RN trained in forensics and she volunteers at a women's shelter. Visit her website at www.loriwilde.com.

Books by Lori Wilde

HARLEQUIN BLAZE

  *The White Star
**The Martini Dares
  †Perfect Anatomy
††Uniformly Hot!
  ‡Stop the Wedding!

To get the inside scoop on Harlequin Blaze and its talented writers, be sure to check out blazeauthors.com.

To my students, past, present and future.
Helping you has made me a better writer.
Thank you.

1

Forward—*Toward the bow*

A PEACOCK COULDN'T have strutted more gloriously than Jeb Whitcomb taking the outdoor makeshift stage. A self-satisfied grin graced his tanned handsome face, his blue eyes crinkled seductively at the corners as he joined the governor at the podium. The sleeves of his white work shirt were rolled up to his elbows, revealing powerful forearms dotted with hair a shade darker than the milk-chocolate locks swept rakishly off his forehead.

"In appreciation of your hard work, dedication and monetary contribution to rebuilding the island of St. Michael's, we are bestowing you with the first Jeb Whitcomb humanitarian award," Governor Freemont announced and passed the gilded trophy to Whitcomb.

From the audience, Haley French, R.N., rolled her eyes. Whitcomb might have everyone else on the island snowed, but Haley saw through the charming smile and sexy swagger. He hadn't really come here to help the residents of St. Michael's; his visit had all been about plumping up his ego. Whenever there was a camera about, Whitcomb was in front of it.

Cameras flashed. Reporters tossed questions. The crowd applauded.

Haley's best friend, Ahmaya Reddy, poked her in the ribs with her elbow. "Don't be rude. Clap."

Halfheartedly, Haley joined in the applause, but she frowned. "He's grandstanding."

Whitcomb launched into what was clearly an off-the-cuff speech.

"He's a bona fide hero," Ahmaya argued. "St. Michael's couldn't have recovered as quickly without him."

"He's self-centered."

"Oh, yes, self-centered people give up a year of their life to rebuild islands they have no connection to."

"That's precisely my point. He has no connection to St. Michael's. Who anointed him our savior? I question his motives. Ever notice how he always has hangers-on following him?"

Ahmaya shrugged. "He's handsome, rich and fun to be around. Who wouldn't want to hang on?"

"Rebuilding an entire island wiped out by a hurricane shouldn't be fun."

"You'd think not, but somehow he managed to get everyone to pull together. That's why he's getting the attention, not to mention the award. His ability to get people to work in harmony."

"He's just doing it for the attention. It strokes his ego."

"So what if he is?" Ahmaya asked. Okay, Haley was being a bit harsh, which was not like her, but

Whitcomb seemed to bring out the worst in her. "The results are the same. People have homes again and essential services have been restored because of Jeb's generosity."

"He's impulsive."

"Oh." A sly smile crossed Ahmaya's face. "I get it."

"Get what?"

"The reason why he rubs you the wrong way."

Haley crossed her arms over her chest, canted her head. "Care to enlighten me?"

"He doesn't live up to your expectations."

"I have no expectations of him."

"No?"

"He's nothing to me."

"I thought you two—"

"We certainly did not." Haley bristled.

"But almost."

Haley's cheeks heated. Yes, she'd almost had sex with Jeb Whitcomb several months back when they'd both served on the hospital rebuilding committee. Thankfully, she had not gone through with it.

"Wait a minute." Ahmaya snapped her fingers. "It's not Jeb who didn't live up to your expectations. It was you. You're mad at him because you violated your own code of ethics when you—"

"Let's stop talking about him, okay?" To get Ahmaya to shut up, she purposefully fixed her attention on the stage.

Jeb had a microphone in his hand. He paced the length of the stage, whipping up the audience with his passionate vision of what St. Michael's could become. Haley knew how dangerous his passion was. He'd had her under his spell, however briefly. He paused in midstride, peered out at the audience and his gaze landed on her.

For one heart-stopping second, their eyes locked and Haley's throat tightened. Darn it, she could not glance away.

Jeb held her pinned to the spot, his eyelids lowered slightly, and his voice took on a seductive quality. Or maybe she had merely imagined it. "Since this is my last day on St. Michael's, I'm having a party on my yacht and everyone is invited," he announced.

A cheer went up from the assembly.

He tossed the microphone to the governor and stalked offstage with a jaunty spring to his step, his entourage of sycophants trailing after him. The crowd gathered around, patting him on the back, trying to shake his hand, but he seemed a man on a mission.

It took Haley a few seconds to realize he was headed toward her. Oh, hell, no.

She spun on her heel. Should be easy enough to disappear in this throng. She rushed forward. Her toe caught on a power cord snaking across the ground and she tripped. *Way to watch where you're going, French.* She put out her palms to catch herself and ended up sprawled on the ground. Oh, she hated being vulnerable.

From behind her came a familiar chuckle. He was already upon her. Before she could scramble up, Jeb's hand went around her waist, his citrusy scent enveloping her as he helped her gently to her feet.

"Easy there, baby," he crooned, bending down to dust the dirt from the knees of her scrubs.

She wrenched away from him, stepped back, breathless and despising herself for it. *Hands off the goods, buster.* Worst of all, she couldn't help meeting his eyes.

There he was standing so close to her in his white shirt, pressed khaki shorts, yachting cap and boat shoes, looking every inch the wealthy windblown yachtsman. Everyone else faded away and it was just the two of them.

His light blue eyes regarded her with a lively sense of humor. It was that sense of humor that had been her undoing. She wasn't going to fall for it. Not twice. No way. No how. He was finally leaving the island. Yay! She'd never have to see him again.

"You're coming to my party, right?" His fingers lightly stroked her upper arm.

No way.

"It wouldn't be a party without you," he went on.

"I've got to wash my hair," she lied. On second thought, why lie? Maybe she would wash her hair. Wash that man right out of it.

"All you need is to lose a few of these pins." His fingers went from her shoulder to her hair, which was pulled up into a tight bun. It was far too intimate of a gesture. He plucked bobby pins from her hair, one by one, and the locks fell loosely to her shoulders. "There, much better."

Haley jerked back, pulse thumping hard. *Oh, no. Do not like this. You are not allowed to like this.*

The expression in his eyes was one of total amusement. He knew he'd made her uncomfortable and he was enjoying himself.

"I'm a stickler for clean hair. I make it a policy to wash it every day." She stuck her chin in the air.

"I know," he murmured, his voice warm and cozy. "You do love your rules."

Who was he to act as if he knew her? Just because they'd almost— Well, never mind what they'd almost done—she was determined to forget it. What really chafed was that *he'd* been the one to pull the plug on their encounter.

"Gotta go." She pointed her feet away from him, but for some unfathomable reason, she did not move.

"I should have known you wouldn't come to my party," he said. "Little Miss Straitlaced."

"Just because I don't want to attend your bacchanal doesn't mean I'm straitlaced."

"Bacchanal?" He sounded amused.

"It's a word. Look it up."

"You're chicken."

She straightened. "I'm not afraid of a thing." *Watch out. Noses grow when lies are told.*

"I disagree. You're terrified of having a good time."

She sniffed. "My idea of a good time and your idea of a good time are two very different things."

"I know. Beating myself up is not my favorite pastime."

She curled her upper lip, determined not to smile back at him. "Well, have a nice party and a safe trip." He'd nailed her, but good. Well, not nailed her in the sexual regard. *Pegged her*—that was better terminology. He'd pegged her. Must hate him for that if nothing else.

"Are you going to miss me when I'm gone?" He leaned down, his grin widening.

All night long. "Not in the least."

"I suppose I asked for that."

"You did."

He batted his eyes at her. "I'm going to miss you."

"Whatever for?"

"You're the only one on this island who keeps me on my toes."

No, sir. She would not let this man turn her into mush. She was better than that. "You want to be on your toes? Wear high heels."

He threw back his head and laughed heartily. "I also love your sense of humor."

"I wasn't trying to be funny." She folded her arms over her chest.

"You're also the only one who doesn't like me, and I can't figure out why."

Haley scoffed. "Not everyone has to like you. Why do you care whether I like you or not?"

"Because I like *you*."

"You like everyone."

"True," he said, taking a step closer. "But not as much as I like you."

She put up her hand like a stop sign. "You don't like me. You like a challenge."

His crystal-blue eyes glittered. "I have to admit, I do enjoy a challenge. The more you resist, the more I want you…" There was a long pause that set her heart to rocking, before he added, "At my party."

"You can want in one hand and spit in the other and see which fills up first."

Jeb laughed long and loud, showing off a row of straight white teeth. That was the problem with the man. He was too perfect and every woman wanted him. Just like the blonde who was sidling up to his elbow and fluttering her false eyelashes at him.

"Your adoring public awaits."

"What?"

She nodded at the woman.

Jeb barely cast the platinum blonde a glance and quickly swung his gaze back to Haley. "Come to my party."

"I don't think so. It takes my hair a really long time to dry," she quipped.

She could not let him know how much he got under her skin. If he knew that he was a major star in her sexual fantasies, she would never hear the end of it. She refused to be like all the other women simpering at his feet.

Yes, he was good-looking. Yes, he was rich. Yes, he had personality and charisma oozing from his pores. Those were exactly the reasons she was not interested. Jeb Whitcomb was a very superficial man.

"It's the last time you'll ever see me." A hangdog expression crawled over his face. "Don't you want to say goodbye?"

"Goodbye." She wriggled her fingers at him.

"The party won't be the same without you."

"You won't miss me."

He canted his head, his eyes drilling into her like lasers. "Ah, see, but that's where you're wrong."

"It's not going to happen, Whitcomb."

He shrugged. "A guy can always dream, can't he?"

"As long as it stays a dream."

He reached out, touched the back of her hand. A shiver ran straight through the middle of her. "I am going to miss you, Haley."

"That makes one of us."

"Ouch." The grin was back as he clutched a hand to his chest. "You play for keeps."

"Don't ever forget it."

The blonde at his elbow edged closer, cleared her throat. "Mr. Whitcomb, I'm from *Metropolitan Magazine* and I want to do a story on you."

Jeb turned to the woman. "Yes?"

With her hand still tingling from his touch, Haley took advantage of his distraction and slipped off into the crowd. Great. She felt like a James Bond martini, shaken and not— Oh, who was she kidding?

She was both shaken *and* stirred.

HALEY STALKED OFF with a purposeful bounce, her honey-colored hair flowing around her shoulders, those blue scrubs stretching across her sexy rump as she marched away.

Jeb grinned, put a palm to the nape of his neck and licked his lips. *Wow, you can park that swing in my backyard anytime.* He tilted his head, honed in on her narrow waist and curvy hips.

His pulse pounded and his body stiffened. In spite of the cool ocean breeze swaying the palm trees, a simmering heat moved through him. He chuffed out a breath, struggling to regain his equilibrium. Truth was, he really would miss her. He enjoyed their sparring matches. She was sassy and saucy and didn't take anything off anyone.

The last person who'd challenged him that same way was his ex-girlfriend, Jackie Birchard. Out of the dozens of girlfriends he'd had, Jackie was the only one to dump him. It made her stand out in the crowd. The one woman he couldn't charm.

That was, until he met Haley. Too bad they'd never hooked up, although they'd come pretty damn close.

Jeb smiled, remembering. He could have gotten her into bed if he'd wanted. When they'd made out on the beach at sunset a few months back, sparks had ignited unlike anything he'd ever felt before, and that was saying something. Haley had wanted him as much as he'd wanted her, maybe even more so, although chances were good that she would never admit it.

But, surprise, surprise, he'd been the one to put a stop to things before they'd completely lost control.

He'd stopped for two reasons. One, he knew Haley would have regretted it the morning after. She was such a stickler for protocol, held herself and others to high standards. Two, he'd been trying to prove to Jackie that she was wrong about him. He wasn't a self-absorbed playboy with no depth of character. He could restrain himself.

No matter how difficult it had been to break that kiss and send Haley home with their desires unfulfilled.

Ah, well, you couldn't win them all, right? It was time to move on. His work on St. Michael's was done. He'd achieved what he'd set out to achieve. He'd helped rebuild the island. He could return home with his head held high.

"About that interview, Mr. Whitcomb," said the blond reporter with a smile that sparkled like prisms.

Matching her smile, Jeb turned and led her away, but he couldn't resist one last glance over his shoulder at Haley.

She paused and looked back.

Their eyes met.

Gotcha! Protest all you want, sweetheart—you do
want me. Boldly, he winked.

Her cheeks reddened and her eyes narrowed in a
scowl. She ducked her head and flounced from his
view, leaving Jeb sorely regretting the night that they'd
never had.

HALEY LAY STRETCHED OUT on her twin bed in the one-
bedroom bungalow she shared with Ahmaya. She was
eating Oreos, twisting the cookies apart and scrap-
ing the white filling off with her front teeth before
gobbling up the dark cookies. Oreos were her go-to
comfort treats when she was stressed or frustrated,
and yes, she knew the drawbacks of de-stressing with
a sugar fix, but when she was feeling like this, she
didn't care.

The quarters were basic and cramped, but a long
sight better than the tent they'd lived in after Hurricane Sylvia. She was trying not to think about Jeb,
but he kept popping into her head at the most un-
wanted times.

Why?

Yes, he was wealthy, handsome and self-confident,
but he was also full of himself and far too free with
his affections. Imagine! He'd called her *baby* and took
the pins out of her hair, and she'd just stood there and
let him. Unexpected goose bumps lifted on her arms
and she hugged herself.

Ahmaya stood in front of the mirrored closet door,
examining her reflection as she got ready for the party.
"What do you think about this skirt?"

"The hem is too short."

"Perfect," Ahmaya purred.

"You're going to wear it anyway?"

"I am. If you think it's too short that means it's exactly the right length."

Haley sat up. "You're saying I'm a prude?"

"Uh-huh, kinda." Ahmaya ran her fingers through her straight, glossy black hair.

"I'm not a prude," she argued against the heavy feeling in the pit of her stomach. Was she? She didn't mean to be; it was just that she had certain principles and she wasn't going to compromise.

"Prove it."

"What?"

"Prove you're not a prude."

"I don't have to prove anything."

"You don't curse."

"So what?"

"Prudes don't curse."

"I believe in having a wide vocabulary. Is that so wrong?"

"Prudish."

"What?" She raised her arms. "I should go around swearing like a sailor to prove I'm not prudish? Okay, then." Haley let loose with a few descriptive curse words.

Ahmaya looked surprised. "I had no idea you knew those words."

"I'm a nurse. I've heard a lot worse than that. It's just that cursing seems so crude and uncivilized."

"Sometimes—" Ahmaya grinned "—it's fun to be uncivilized."

"If you say so."

"Prude."

"Are we back to that?"

"It's the truth of your being."

"I don't think *prude* is the right word. *Prudent,* if you wish, but not *prudish.*"

"Hmm." Ahmaya stepped into a pair of mile-high stilettos. "Prove it."

"I just did."

"Not by cursing, by coming with me to Jeb's party. I need a wing woman."

"You don't need a wing woman."

"Everyone needs a wing woman."

"Call Jessie. I'm sure she'd go."

"She's stuck working second shift."

"Ahmaya, I don't want to go."

"But you're the one with a car."

"It's only a half mile. You can ride your bike."

"In this?" Ahmaya swept a dramatic hand at her sexy outfit. She had a point. Jimmy Choo didn't pedal well. Her friend dropped on her knees in front of Haley, pressed her palms together. "Please, please, please. I'll do the crash-cart checks for you all month."

Haley sighed. "You know parties aren't my thing."

"Seriously, it's great that you're all into altruistic causes and saving people and everything, but you can't work or think about work 24/7. You need to lighten up. Let your hair down."

That remark had Haley remembering how Jeb had pulled the bobby pins from her hair. She suppressed a shiver. He'd kept her bobby pins. It would serve him right if she went to his party and demanded the return of her bobby pins.

"You are the dullest twenty-seven-year-old I know." Ahmaya pouted.

Ouch! That hurt.

Haley considered self-discipline her strong suit, not a flaw. It was what had gotten her through nursing school with a 4.0 grade-point average. An accomplishment she was very proud of.

"One little bitty party isn't going to kill you. Everyone is going to be there. Look at it as a networking opportunity." Ahmaya batted her long, dark lashes. "Pretty please?"

"Oh, all right, but I'm only staying for one drink and then I'm out of there."

"You'll drink really slowly, right?"

"An hour. I'll stay an hour. If you're ready to go in an hour, you can leave with me. If you're not, then you'll have to find your own way home."

Ahmaya's face dissolved into a happy smile and she extended her hand. "Deal."

Huffing out a sigh, Haley shook her hand.

"Now," Ahmaya said, "we have to find you something sexy to wear."

"No, we don't. Jeans and a T-shirt will do just fine."

Ahmaya looked aghast. "Shut your mouth. This is a par-*tay.* You're not going looking like a schlub."

"I came here with the Red Cross and I stayed to work. I have scrubs and jeans and that's it."

"Ah." Ahmaya's eyes glistened. "But *I* have party clothes. My sister sent me a big box of them last month."

"You wear a size four."

"You're not that much bigger than me. I bet we can squeeze you into my blue Ann Taylor Loft spaghetti strap. Ann Taylor sizes run big, and blue is your color." Ahmaya dug in her closet, found the dress, tossed it to Haley. "The dress is a little bland for my taste anyway. Should be right up your alley."

"I'm not much for florals. Too girly."

"No excuses. Try it on." Ahmaya sank her hands on her hips.

Reluctantly, Haley stripped off her scrubs and put on the dress. It hugged her curves and the hem fell halfway up her thigh. *Hello, where's the burlesque stage? Gypsy Rose Lee is in the house.* She tugged at the bottom of the dress, trying to lengthen it. "It's too short."

"You've got dynamite legs. Why are you so scared to show them?"

"I'm not scared. Just not interested in looking like a hoochie mama."

"You're saying I'm a hoochie mama?"

"The dress isn't snug on you and you're two inches shorter than I am."

"Celebrate your curves, Haley. I'm jealous."

"It's too tight in the boobs."

"It's perfect. That's the way a sexy dress is supposed to fit."

"I'll need a strapless bra."

Ahmaya's eyes danced mischievously. "Go braless."

"My nipples will show."

"I have Nippies you can wear. No more excuses."

"What are Nippies?"

"Gawd, do you live under a rock? They're nipple covers."

"I live on a hurricane-devastated island. My concerns run more toward basic human necessities than fashion."

"You can say that again. Can you for once not be a Debbie Downer?"

That startled her. "Am I really a killjoy?"

"Yeah, kinda. Not everyone lives by your work-work-work credo, and you know, sometimes people need something fun to take their minds off the bad things that have happened. Jeb totally gets that."

Her friend's comment stopped Haley in her tracks. It wasn't the first time she'd heard that she was too focused on hard work and doing things by the book. Did everyone think she was a hard-ass? Yes, she was very careful by nature and thorough in forming her opinions, and she had high principles. Why was that a bad thing? Why did she so often feel out of step with others her age?

"Haley, if you're not perfect every minute of the day, the world won't come to an end," Ahmaya said, her voice softening. "Please just try to have fun tonight. Will you promise me that?"

She really did want to fit in. Wanted people to like her. "I'll try, but the main reason I don't want to go is that Jeb Whitcomb will be there."

"Of course he'll be there. It's his party."

"He's just so cocky. He thinks that all women want to fall at his feet."

"Most of them do."

"Not me."

"Do you really want to make him suffer?"

That intrigued her. "How would I do that?"

"Show up looking gorgeous. Let him see what he'll never have. Rub it in."

Hmm. She liked that. Little Miss Sadist. "Okay, I'll do it."

"Yay." Ahmaya clapped. "Now, will you let me do your makeup?"

Haley started to resist—Ahmaya had a tendency to overdo makeup application—but she quickly thought better of it. She was determined to prove she could be a party animal just like everyone else, even if it killed her.

But most of all, she wanted to give Jeb Whitcomb a good-riddance send-off he wouldn't forget.

2

Luff—*The flapping motion of the sailcloth when a sail is undertrimmed*

JEB WAS IN HIS ELEMENT. He loved throwing parties, loved crowds. Having people around amped him up, fed his energy.

It wasn't even sunset and the party was already rocking. Wang Chung was urging "Everybody Have Fun Tonight" from the sound system. People were bobbing and weaving to the beat. The bartender he'd hired was imitating Tom Cruise moves from *Cocktail*. The yacht overflowed, people spilling out onto the gangplank and dock. The caterers dished up delectable canapés—prawn spring rolls, Thai chicken skewers, langoustine pastry puffs, smoked-salmon crisps, mini Yorkshire pudding with roast beef and horseradish, and mushrooms stuffed with lump crab meat. Japanese paper lanterns and flickering citronella candles provided intimate lighting. The air smelled salty and calm.

He stood smiling, dressed in a blue button-down

silk shirt, chino slacks and deck shoes without socks, a tumbler of finely aged Scotch and water in his hand. Great turnout. Then again, the turnout for his parties was always great.

But one person was missing. The person he most wanted to see.

You really didn't think she'd show, did you?

No, he hadn't. Why did she snub him so vigorously? Why did he care so much to begin with? He was supposed to resist the allure of other women so he could win Jackie back. His ex-girlfriend would have to be impressed with all he'd accomplished on St. Michael's. He'd proven he wasn't a dilettante and that he was serious about helping others.

The hospital administrator came over to thank him again for his contributions. Jeb leaned in, pretended to listen intently, but his gaze kept straying to the dock, watching the arriving guests.

No Haley.

What was the big deal? He should be happy to have that contentious female out of his life for good. He would be on his way home to Florida tomorrow. He should be thinking about Jackie. She would be so surprised to see him.

Yes! Going home. He missed Miami and he was turning flips at the thought of seeing Jackie again and showing her how he'd changed, but he couldn't help wishing he could have said goodbye to Haley. He would miss the way she challenged him at every turn. Not too many people did that to him.

Jackie did.

It had just been so long since he'd seen Jackie that he was imbuing Haley with his ex-girlfriend's traits.

That was all this was. That was all it could be, because he'd given up being a ladies' man and he was damned proud of his restraint.

A year.

It had been a year since he'd been with a woman. His longest record since he'd lost his virginity at sixteen. *See, Jackie, I have changed!*

The governor and his wife joined Jeb's conversation with the hospital administrator. Jeb winked at the wife, a dumpy woman in her mid-fifties wearing a colorful muumuu. "You're looking beautiful tonight, Mrs. Freemont."

She blushed like a girl and ducked her head. "You're such an outrageous flirt."

From eight to eighty, most women were so easy to charm. Look them straight in the eye, pay them a compliment and mean it. That was the essential part. You truly had to love women. Add a conspiratorial wink and they were putty.

All except for Jackie.

And Haley.

"You don't have drinks," Jeb said to the Freemonts. "Let me rectify that right now." He motioned for one of the waiters roving through the crowd with trays of hors d'oeuvres to come over. He gave their order to the waiter, turned back to pick up the thread of the conversation when his attention was immediately snagged by a leggy honey-blonde sauntering up the gangplank.

She wore a skimpy little blue dress with tiny white flowers scattered over the material, and her breasts moved with such a pert bounce he had to assume she was not wearing a bra.

Instantly, his body lit up.

His gaze trailed from the blue four-inch stiletto sandals on her delicate little feet, up the length of those amazing calves and back to the nip of her narrow waist to the boldly unharnessed breasts, and finally, he glanced at her face.

His heart did a double take.

No way! This could not be Haley French looking like a supermodel with her perfectly arched eyebrows and glossy pink lips.

His eyes bugged out and his tongue stuck to the roof of his mouth. He knew she was pretty, yes indeed, but he had absolutely no idea she could look like this. Stunning.

"Excuse me," he said smoothly to the Freemonts and the hospital administrator, then set down his drink and made a beeline straight for Haley.

Her eyes widened and she reached for the elbow of the dark-haired girl beside her. She said something short and succinct to her friend, shook her head, spun on her heel and hurried back down the gangplank.

"Wait!" Jeb called, pushing through the crowd.

But Haley didn't even glance around. Her friend stood on the gangplank looking bewildered.

"Jeb, hey, I've been wanting to speak to you," someone said.

"Great party." A beautiful woman clutched at his arm.

A man clapped him on the shoulder. "We're going to miss you on St. Michael's."

"Excuse me, excuse me." Jeb shook off the people. Why was he so desperate to prevent her from leaving?

He blew past Haley's friend, reached the end of the gangplank. Haley was a good twenty feet ahead of him. She was already off the dock and climbing the stairs to the marina parking lot.

"Haley!"

She didn't turn around.

He was running now. *Definitely uncool. Ruining your image, dude. Stop it.*

Jeb reached the bottom of the stairs just as Haley crested them. "Baby, don't go."

She stopped in midstep and spun around to glower at him. One sexy gam perched on the landing, the other on the step below. "Excuse me?"

"Baby, please don't go."

"Baby? Did you just call me *baby?*"

He shrugged, chagrined. "Sorry. Figure of speech."

"Do I look like an infant to you?"

"No, ma'am. Not in any way, shape or form."

Slowly, she came back down the steps toward him, her eyes blazing fire. His pulse hammered hotly through his veins. "The word *baby* is also often used as a term of endearment between lovers," she said.

"Uh-huh." He nodded.

"Are we lovers?"

"Unfortunately, no." What was he doing? Jackie was the one for him. He was trying not to seduce other women, and for a whole year, he'd been a very good boy. He should just tell Haley goodbye and go back to the party.

"I am not an infant and we are not lovers, correct?"

"Correct."

"Then under no circumstances are you to call me *baby.* Got it?"

He gave a jaunty salute. "Got it. No *baby.* Not now, not ever. The word is stricken from my vocabulary."

"Good. Even among lovers I find the word off-putting. Infantilizing each other isn't the way to build a mature, loving bond."

"You have strong opinions about it."

"I do."

"You really don't like me all that much, do you?"

"Not especially."

"Why did you come tonight?"

"My friend Ahmaya needed a wing woman and a ride. She doesn't have a car."

"You were just going to go off and leave her?"

For one second, she looked shamefaced, but quickly recovered. "Ahmaya's a big girl. She can take care of herself."

"And yet, you came with her." Jeb raked his gaze over Haley. "Looking like that, I might add."

A pink blush crept up her neck. "It's Ahmaya's dress."

"You're stunning."

"Oh, I feel so special," she said snidely. "I bet you said that to only a couple dozen women today."

"More like a baker's dozen," he teased.

Her shoulders relaxed a little at that and a tiny smile briefly lit her lips. Small victory. With Haley, he'd take his triumphs where he could get them.

"Are you still planning on running away?"

"I'm not running away."

"Seems to me you are."

"I can't run in these shoes. I was walking away or, more accurately, hobbling away."

"Why?"

"I don't like parties."

"Why not?"

"They're too crowded. I don't like crowds."

"Uh, you forget I saw you in action in those relief camps right after Hurricane Sylvia. The tents were packed tighter than sardine cans and you were right in the middle of it."

"That was different. I was helping people."

"C'mon back to the party," he coaxed. "I'll let you give the Heimlich maneuver if anyone chokes on a canapé."

There was that brief smile again.

His heart gave a strange bunny hop. He held out a hand. "C'mon."

They stood there a moment; Haley posed on the top steps, Jeb at the bottom, groveling, palm outstretched.

"Don't leave me hanging, ba—" He almost said *baby* but stopped in the nick of time.

"Why should I come back to your party?"

"For one thing, you're a good friend. Ahmaya needs you."

"Low blow."

"I'll use any tool in the arsenal."

"Why?"

"Why what?"

"Why do you care so much if I'm at your party or not?"

It was a very good question. He didn't have a glib answer handy and ended up just blurting out the truth. "I've got enough yes-men and yes-women around me. I need someone who knows how to luff a sail."

"A what?"

"There are no brakes on a sailboat. The only way to slow down is to luff the sail. That means to undertrim the sail so it doesn't catch any wind."

"In other words, I'm a brake, huh?"

"Well, you know you are a stickler for rules, etiquette, proper behavior and all that." He waved a hand.

"A wet blanket."

"I didn't say that."

"A Debbie Downer."

"I didn't say that, either."

"Why would you want a brake at your party? Parties are supposed to be go, go, go. No-holds-barred. Looks like you'd want an accelerator, not a brake."

"Don't be offended by the brake comment. A brake is a good thing," he said. "A brake is very necessary. A brake keeps you safe."

"Like a mother?"

He shoved fingers through his hair. "This isn't going well, is it?"

"Not in the least." She folded her arms over her chest, but the smile was back and stayed a fraction of a second longer this time.

"Come luff my sails, Haley."

She hesitated. Ha! He had her.

"You're already dressed to impress. Why waste it?" he cajoled.

"I don't know why I'm even considering this."

"'Cause part of you doesn't really want to spend tonight all alone washing your hair."

"I don't mind being by myself."

Man, she was a hard nut to crack. "Okay," he said. "But you don't know what you're missing." Taking a calculated risk, he turned to go.

"Wait."

He grinned, stopped, but did not turn back around. "Yes?"

"I *am* pretty hungry. I'll stay for a bite to eat." The sound of her mincing down the metal stairs in her stilettos rang out into the twilight.

He bent his arm at the elbow, signaling for her to take it. To his surprise, she did.

"Only because I'm wearing high heels," she said, reading his mind as she slipped her arm through his.

Her touch ignited a firestorm inside him. Jeb gulped. Good thing he was sailing out tomorrow— one more day around Haley and there was no telling what might happen.

HALEY HAD NO IDEA WHY she'd allowed smooth-talking Jeb Whitcomb to coax her into coming back to his party.

Partially, it was true that she was hungry and hated to cook for just herself, plus, there was her promise to Ahmaya, but there was another part of her that she didn't really want to poke. The part that *liked* being around Jeb.

The minute they reached the deck of his sailing yacht, Haley let go of his arm. She was disturbed to find herself breathless.

"What would you like to drink?" Jeb asked.

"You don't have to get my drink."

"It's no problem." He lifted a finger at a white-gloved waiter waiting at the ready.

Haley supposed a lot of women fell for the master-and-commander routine. Your every wish was his command. Seductive, for sure, but she mistrusted anything that wasn't hard-won.

The waiter appeared at his side.

"Could you please bring Miss French a..." Jeb looked at her expectantly.

"Diet cola."

"Seriously?"

"I don't drink."

"Not ever?"

"Rarely. New Year's Eve. Wedding toasts. That kind of thing."

"This is my going-away party."

"So?"

"You're not going to toast my journey?"

"I can toast with diet cola."

He got a knowing look on his face. "Aha."

"What?"

He shrugged. "Nothing."

"The 'aha' meant something."

"It's not important."

"Then why did you say it?"

The corner of his mouth tipped up. "I've figured out something about you."

She pulled her lips downward. "And what is that?"

"You're afraid of losing control."

"What's wrong with that?"

"I never said anything was wrong with it. Just had a lightbulb moment."

"I like to keep my wits about me."

"Make an exception," he said.

"You want me witless?"

"Maybe."

"Why?"

"To prove you can let your hair down."

"I don't have to prove a thing to you."

He leaned closer. "No, but wouldn't it be fun to stop thinking so much for once and simply let go?"

"Five minutes ago you were telling me you needed someone who knew how to luff a sail."

"If the sailcloth stayed luffed, you'd never set sail."

"Nothing wrong with dry land."

"You're not a sailor?"

"Landlubber all the way. That's me." She groaned.

The waiter cleared his throat.

"You're holding up the poor man," Jeb said. "What'll you have? And no diet coke unless it has rum in it."

She thought about sticking to her guns, but it was easier just to give in, and at some point, you couldn't fight everything, right? *Pick your battles, Haley. Everything is not worthy of a crusade.* She recited her mother's frequent advice. "White wine, something with a low alcohol content and sweet."

"Uh," he said sounding mildly amused. "I had you pegged for something tart, like a salty dog."

"What's a salty dog?"

"Grapefruit juice and vodka with a salted rim."

"When it comes to alcohol, the sweeter the better." She crinkled her nose. "I don't like the taste."

"Bring her a glass of Luccio Moscato d'Asti," he told the waiter.

The waiter actually bowed, clicked his patent leather heels and departed for the open bar.

"What's Moscato whatever?"

"Light, white dessert wine, five percent alcohol. Couldn't get a kitten drunk on it. You'll love the stuff."

"Sounds perfect." She spied Ahmaya in the center of a clot of men—so much for hope of rescue on that score.

"Come." Jeb took her by the elbow and escorted her toward the buffet.

She wanted to resist out of general principle—he was far too proprietary—but the deck was crowded, and in these ridiculous stilettos, it was nice to have him threading the needle to the food. But what disconcerted her most was the feel of his skin against hers. Just like she'd enjoyed that kiss he'd given her on the beach several months back. Which, if she were being honest, was at the heart of why she wanted to avoid him.

He handed her a plate and the waiter brought her drink. Solicitously, Jeb held the wineglass for her while she filled her plate. The gentlemanly shtick was all part of his seduction ritual, no doubt. *Don't fall for his courteous manners. It's a trap.*

"You're not going to have anything to eat?" she asked him.

"When I eat, I'm not giving my guests my full attention."

"Well, feel free to mingle." She waved him off. "Don't let me hold you back."

"Ah, but you're one of my guests. I want to make sure all your needs are met."

Her stomach grumbled, so she loaded up on food while he waited, and then he guided her down three steps to bench seating on the lower deck. Two people were sitting there, but he went over and whispered something to them and they got up. He turned to smile and waved triumphantly at the vacated seats.

"You ran them off?"

"I politely asked if they'd mind giving up their seats for a lady whose feet were hurting."

"Hey, I can eat just fine standing up."

Jeb sat and patted the spot next to him. "Please, have a seat, Haley."

The way he said her name, as if it were the most elegant sound on earth, sent tingles zipping through her. Reluctantly, she sat and perched her plate on her knees, which she kept firmly pressed together in the too-short dress. Instead of meeting his gaze, she concentrated on pulling a morsel of chicken off a wooden skewer.

"I'm glad you came tonight."

"That makes one of us."

"You love busting my chops."

She grinned. She did.

"How's the wine?"

"Haven't tasted it yet." She took a sip. Ooh, it went down sweet and smooth. "I like it. Reminds me of Kool-Aid."

"Wow, something you approve of. Duly noted."

"No need to note it. This is the last time we'll ever see each other."

"You sound happy about that."

Not happy. Relieved. And grateful that she'd managed to avoid his charms and stay out of his bed, although she'd had a near miss.

He reached out to touch her hand. "I'm going to miss you, Haley. I've never met anyone quite like you."

She slipped her arm away. "Great puff pastries. Kudos to the caterers."

"I'll pass along your compliments to the chef."

An awkward silence passed between them.

"You're one of the hardest workers I've ever had the pleasure to know," he said.

"Thank you." What was he getting at?

"And I admire how straightforward you are. No beating around the bush."

"Speaking of that." She dusted off her fingers with a napkin. "Let me just set you straight. There's no way I'm spending the night with you. Not if it were my last night on earth."

"Whew." Laughing, he leaned back in his seat and wiped a palm over his forehead in mock relief.

Whew? Haley scowled.

"Because the last thing in the world I ever want to do is have sex with you," he said.

She stared at him, stunned, her jaw unhinged. He did not want to have sex with her? "Excuse me?"

"Don't get me wrong. It's not because you're not desirable, because you most certainly are in a tough-girl, nothing-touches-me-emotionally kind of way."

"Then what the hell is this full-court press about? Begging me to come to your party, getting me food and wine, *touching* me like you mean business."

He held up a palm. "Wait a minute. Let me get this straight—you want me to want you, but you're not about to sleep with me?"

Haley pursed her lips guiltily. Yeah, well, sorta. "I want to be the one woman who won't fall at your feet."

His grin turned wolfish. "You almost did."

"But I didn't."

"Only because *I* called it off."

"I would have called it off. You just beat me to it."

"We'll never know, will we?"

She put her plate aside. She really wanted more of

those crab-stuffed mushrooms, but she did not want to sit here with Jeb Whitcomb any longer. "You are driving me bonkers."

"Right back atcha, baby."

"Don't call me *baby!*" How was it that this man could ruffle her so easily? She hated that.

"Why not? You're acting like one. I was trying to pay you a compliment and you got all twisted off for no reason. You have a tendency to do that."

"Yeah? Well, you have a tendency to believe you're God's gift to women. News flash, you're nothing but a rich frat boy swooping in with your money to make yourself feel good."

"What's wrong with that? I feel good, people get the help they need."

"Because you sail away to your fancy life, leaving people longing for you."

His smile turned knowing and he lowered his voice. "Are you longing for me, Haley?"

"Yes, longing for you to be gone." Wine in hand, she flounced away.

3

Safety harness—*Personal gear that attaches to a
tether to keep the person on board*

JEB TOOK A LONG PULL off his Scotch and water; the
synapses in his brain were alight with lusty and inappropriate impulses. He'd pissed her off.

Oh, she was gorgeous when she was mad and she
had the world's cutest scowl, hands down. He followed
her up the steps, back to the bridge. She circled the
boat.

He licked his lips.

She ended up talking to one of her coworkers starboard, but every now and then, she'd dart a glance
in his direction. When their eyes met, she'd quickly
glance away. *Can't handle the heat, huh, angel?*

Corner her. Kiss her, hissed one of those lusty, inappropriate impulses.

Nope. No way. He'd lasted this long without giving
in. He could certainly last one more night. Haley deserved much better than a quick one-night stand, but
even a pious man had his share of sexual fantasies,

right? And when it came to the pious spectrum, Jeb slid to the not-so-much side of the scale.

She was unlike the sophisticated society women that he usually dated, women who could shrug in and out of an affair like their designer clothes. Haley was honest and down-to-earth and direct, and he was a jerk for even entertaining the fantasies dancing around in his head.

He made the rounds, talking to his party guests, but no matter where he was on the boat, his gaze was drawn back to her again and again. A full moon climbed the sky, setting the mood and tugging at the tides. Haley stood in shadows with her head tilted up, bathing that side of her face in moonlight, and she let out a light laugh that stirred his desire.

Do something. Move. Drink. Eat. Talk to your other guests. Just stop staring at her!

He went toward her. She stood with her back against the mainsail mast, her spine as straight as the post. She had great posture, shoulders squared and alert.

People stood around her, drinks in hand, but he saw none of them. Moonlight glinted off her eyes; her lips were painted deep pink. He realized it was the first time he ever remembered seeing her wear lipstick. The wind ruffled her hair, which for once was not pulled into a stern ponytail or tight bun. The breeze molded the dress to her slender figure, hugging her hips and stopping several inches above her knees.

His mammalian brain whispered, *Claim her.*

Resist. You are not going to succumb. One more night and you'll be out to sea. Within a week, you'll be holding Jackie in your arms and the wait will be worth it.

Love the one you're with, prodded the most primal part of him.

He snuffed that out.

Or at least tried to.

Haley was watching him warily.

He moved closer.

She slunk away.

Seeing her in this environment—*his* environment—was novel and exciting, and he simply reacted, moving forward as she slipped away from him behind other guests.

The chase was on.

The part of his DNA that was thousands of years old stirred, eager for the hunt. His body quivered and his heart hammered against his rib cage. All his senses were aroused.

His civilized veneer vanished. Raw, aching need took over. Need so strong it scared him.

Back off! Wake up. Snap out of it.

Treacherous body.

He shook his head but could not seem to stave off the sense of urgency shoving his blood through his veins. He was a lion and she was the most beautiful lioness on the plains. She mesmerized him and he was aware of everything about her. It was disorienting, this acute sense of awareness.

His muscles were tensed, the hairs on his arms raised, a thrill shivered through his nerve endings. He felt well and truly alive, but the jolt was nerve-frazzling and worrisome.

Around and around the boat they went, Jeb pursuing, Haley fleeing. It was fun and he was quite enjoying himself, even though he knew nothing would come of this strange cat-and-mouse game. Didn't want anything to come of it.

Until a group of people cornered him for a toast and Haley gave him the slip.

HEART IN HER THROAT, a helpless smile on her face, Haley hid behind a large man to catch her breath and then rushed down the steps as best she could to the lower deck. What was this weird game they were playing and why was she playing it? Why didn't she just leave?

Why? Because Jeb had lit a fire inside her that scared her silly. Being with him was like driving a Ferrari on the Autobahn with a learner's permit. Roadkill. She'd been there before. Refused to be there again.

She had to get off this boat. Coming to the lower deck had been a mistake. He could corner her down here.

Alarmed by that thought, she moved to climb the steps but she wasn't accustomed to stilettos. It took more skill than one might suppose. She tripped and nose-dived forward, wine splashing out of her glass. She would have hit the deck if a masculine hand hadn't reached out to catch her.

"Are you okay?"

She glanced up to see Rick Armand, a respiratory therapist who worked at St. Michael's General Hospital. He'd asked her out several times, but she'd put him off. She considered him a bit smarmy with his oversize porn-star moustache and the way he clicked his tongue and used his fingers like pistols, pretending he was shooting her. Still, she let him rescue her from Jeb. "I'm fine."

"You lost your drink," Rick said. "Let's get you another."

She was about to say no, when she glanced back to see Jeb giving her the eye. "Yes, that sounds good. Make it a salty dog, please," she said extra loudly so Jeb would hear.

Rick took her empty wineglass and gave it to a passing waiter. "Would you like to come with me?"

Yes…yes, she would.

She accepted Rick's hand and allowed him to lead her to the bar. It took everything she had in her not to look back to see the reaction on Jeb's face. She wouldn't give him the satisfaction of knowing she cared what he was thinking about her going off with Rick.

As they stepped up to the bar, Rick placed a hand to the small of her back. Haley moved sideways and Rick dropped his hand. "Salty dog for the lady," he told the bartender. "And I'll have a beer."

"Thank you," she told him.

"I've never seen you looking like this," Rick said, raking a lascivious gaze over her. "I like it."

"Moment of temporary insanity," Haley mumbled and tugged at the hem. A bandanna had more material in it. How did Ahmaya wear these skimpy dresses without feeling overexposed?

"I like it."

The bartender placed their drinks on the bar. Rick reached over, plucked a pink flamingo stir stick from the holder, dropped it into Haley's drink and stirred the salty dog before handing it over to her.

"The alcohol tends to settle to the bottom. You have to stir it to make sure it's completely mixed. Don't want that last swallow to be pure alcohol. Might go straight to your head." Rick leered as if that was exactly what he was hoping would happen.

See, this sort of thing was precisely why she didn't like wearing short skirts and stilettos. It had guys dripping all over her.

"Thanks for watching out for me," she said sarcastically and stirred her drink vigorously.

"My pleasure." Rick showed a row of small, crowded teeth. Shark.

What was she doing here with this dweeb? Oh, yeah, avoiding Jeb. She looked around for him, didn't see him. Thank heavens.

They stepped away from the bar, walking to the back of the boat. Aft, she thought it was called. She touched the straw to her lips, took a swallow of the salty dog. Not bad. Tangy. Salty. Tart. She took another sip. Hmm, on second thought, it had a weird aftertaste she didn't really like. Maybe she could dump the drink overboard.

"Your eyes sparkle in this lighting," Rick said. "And with the full moon behind you, the night is picture-perfect."

"Um."

Rick started telling her about the souped-up Camaro he'd ordered and was having shipped in from the States, expounding at length on exactly how much he'd paid for it. Like, really, who cared if he'd blown a year's salary on a car?

He pitched forward. "You're not drinking your drink."

"It tastes a little weird."

"Do you want me to get you something else?"

"No, I'm fine."

Rick held up his beer mug. "A toast?"

"To what?"

"To seeing people in a different light."

Why not? "To seeing people in a different light," she repeated.

They clinked glasses. Feeling obligated, Haley took another swallow. What was that weird aftertaste? It was just supposed to be grapefruit juice, vodka and salt.

"And to a beautiful night." Rick raised his mug again.

"To a beautiful night." This time, she barely sipped the drink. Okay, she was definitely going to have to pour it overboard when Rick wasn't looking.

She meandered toward the edge, but before she could get there, a woozy sensation hit her and she wobbled on her heels. Whoa, those salty dogs sneaked up on you.

"Are you all right?" Rick loomed over her.

Back off, dude. "I'm fine." She didn't want him to know she was feeling tipsy. "I just need to, um…go powder my nose." *And get away from you.*

It occurred to her that she was spending the night running away from men. She knew that most women would love to have two guys vying over them, but Haley found it annoying more than anything else.

"Could you excuse me?" she asked, pushing her drink at him.

He curled his hand around the glass. "Sure, I'll be waiting right here."

Making sure to take careful steps, she maneuvered through the crowd. She longed to go home, but she couldn't drive like this. Not with her head swirling. She'd go to the restroom, splash some cool water on her face and then go find Ahmaya and see if she was in any shape to drive them home.

Seriously, she was such a lightweight. A few sips of wine and a quarter of a salty dog and her knees were buckling.

Carefully, she made her way from the bridge to the main deck. The party was in full swing. People were dancing all over the place to The Red Hot Chili Peppers singing "Under the Bridge." How appropriate. She realized that Jeb must have handpicked songs for the evening. Slick. What else would she expect from him?

"Bathroom?" she asked a woman she knew from the hospital.

"The one on this level is occupied, but I heard there's an en suite in Jeb's cabin on the lower deck."

"Thanks," Haley said. Wow, was she actually slurring her words? This was why she didn't drink. She could not hold her liquor.

As she clung to the stair railing that led to the lowest deck, her head spun so wildly that she had to stop several times and take a deep breath. Finally, after what felt like a hundred years, she stumbled into the bedroom.

Jeb's bedroom.

A strange feeling passed through her as she stared at the bed and vividly imagined herself in it with Jeb. *Oh, knock it off.* She had to get into that bathroom and put some cold water on her face.

She sank against the door, clicked it locked in case anyone else wandered this way. She needed privacy until the dizziness passed. After a minute, she lurched toward the bathroom door. Heat swamped her body. Her mouth was like a desert. And those damn stilettos were anchors on her feet.

This didn't feel right. Sure, she was a lightweight drinker, but this…this was more than being tipsy. This felt *wrong*.

Her vision blurred. She couldn't think. *Help!*

She heard a knock on the door.

"Haley?" It was Rick.

He was the last person she wanted to see.

The door handle rattled. "Haley, are you in there?"

She might not want to see him, but she was feeling very weird and maybe he could help her. She opened her mouth to answer, but belatedly, it occurred to her that Rick might have put something in her drink. The salty dog had a funky aftertaste and he'd stirred it before he'd passed it to her.

Had she been drugged? How naive was she to have trusted him?

Her heart thundered in her chest as the truth of it hit her. Rick was a predator prowling outside, waiting to pounce. Thankfully, she'd had the presence of mind to lock the bedroom door.

The bathroom was so close and yet seemed a hundred miles away. Screw it. She was going to lie right down here on Jeb's bed for a couple of minutes, just until the dizziness passed and Rick went away, and then she'd go find Jeb and tell him what she suspected had happened to her.

Jeb would know how to handle that lowlife Rick. A charming playboy Jeb might be, but oddly enough she trusted him. Beneath that party-hearty attitude, he *was* a good guy. She had to admit that.

Satisfied with her plan, Haley flopped headfirst onto the mattress and that was the last thing she remembered.

THE LAST GUEST LEFT at 3:00 a.m., as the cleaning crew Jeb had hired swept down the deck. By the time he paid the cleaners, the caterers and the parking-lot attendants, he was so exhausted he could barely keep his eyes open. The party had been a resounding success, but even in the midst of that knowledge, he was disappointed, because at some point during the night, Haley had slipped away without saying goodbye.

He'd been on the lookout for her, but hadn't managed to see her again after she'd gone off with Mustache Rick. He'd found Rick, who was frantically searching for Haley, so he figured she'd given the smarmy respiratory therapist the slip, not him. Still, he would have liked one last conversation with her.

Never mind. He had other things to think about. Like getting home to Miami to see Jackie. He couldn't believe it had been a year since they'd spoken, and he was eager to see her again and show her how much he'd changed.

He thought about his last conversation with Jackie, when she'd broken up with him. It had come as a shocker—because no woman had ever broken up with him. Jackie had been on her father's research ship, the *Sea Anemone,* and he'd sailed up and tried to get her to blow off work and go sailing with him.

"Some of us work for a living, Jeb," Jackie had said, clearly irritated with him.

"I work for a living," he'd protested, giving her his biggest smile and an endearing wink.

"When was the last time you built something?"

Hmm, well, it had been over a year since he'd completed the Miami Beach condos, but everyone knew the Florida real-estate market was in the toilet. His strategy was simply to wait it out and have a good time while doing it. "I'll be ready when the market turns around."

"You have the luxury of waiting. Most people don't, Jeb. You squander your time."

"I don't see things that way."

"I do and I just don't think this relationship is working. We're too different."

That comment had smacked him upside the head. "I can change."

"Seriously? You come from money. It's all you've ever known. You don't really have to work. You're a playboy at heart. I mean, c'mon, just look at the name of your yacht. *Feelin' Nauti.* You summed yourself up quite neatly."

"But don't we have a lot of fun together?" he'd wheedled.

"Yes, that's precisely the problem. All we do is have fun together."

"What's wrong with that?" he'd asked, puzzled.

"Nothing as long as it's in small doses. But my life is ninety percent work, ten percent play. You, on the other hand, are completely the reverse. Ten percent work, ninety percent play. It's not a lifestyle I desire."

That had thrown him for a loop. All his life he'd been complimented on his ability to light up any room he walked into and now here was Jackie telling him that wasn't necessarily a good thing. "So let me get this straight. You're breaking up with me because I'm too much fun to be around?"

"Precisely."

"I'll work."

"Prove it."

"How?"

"Go do something useful."

"Like what?"

"I don't know. Find someone to help. Find something bigger than yourself to be a part of. Figure it out."

"If I do that, will you give me a second chance?"

"Jeb—"

"Please," he said, "don't cut off all hope."

She sighed. "All right. I'll give you a year. If you can get involved with something meaningful and prove to me you've changed, we'll see."

"You won't regret it," he said, but she'd already turned back to her research materials.

The first thing he'd done was change the name of his boat to *Second Chance,* even though it was supposedly bad luck to change the name of a boat. The very next day, Hurricane Sylvia had churned up the Atlantic and a few days later slammed into St. Michael's. Bad luck for St. Michael's, but Jeb had taken it as a sign and he'd headed out to help rebuild the devastated island.

Jeb smiled smugly. Jackie had given him a much-needed wakeup call, and she was going to be so impressed at how he'd changed.

He shut off the lights, blew out the candles and stood on the deck in the moonlight. He was damned proud of what he'd done. He'd gone from thinking only of himself to putting others first, and he was so grateful to Jackie for setting him on this path. He couldn't wait to tell her about it.

Bed. It was time to go to bed, but he didn't have the energy to head down to his bunk on the lower deck.

He stretched, yawned, completely exhausted. His eyelids were heavy. He walked to the blue-and-white-striped bridge hammock, stretched out, cupped his head in his palms and stared up at the stars.

"I'm coming home a changed man, Jackie," he murmured and instantly fell into a deep sleep.

4

Crab—*To compensate for current or leeway by correcting the heading to one side of the actual course*

THE SOUND OF HIS CELL PHONE announcing a text message woke Jeb at dawn. Bleary-eyed, he pulled a palm down his face, blinked at the pink rays of sun pushing up over the crystal-blue water.

Ding.

The cell phone in his back pocket reminded him about the text.

He blew out his breath, dropped his feet over one side of the hammock and fished in his back pocket for his phone. The text was from Jackie. His pulse leaped and he grinned widely.

Until he read the message.

To our closest friends and family. You are invited to the Fourth of July wedding of Coast Guard Lieutenant Commander Scott Marcus Everly and Jacqueline

Michele Birchard at 4:00 p.m. aboard the *Sea Anemone* docked at Wharf 16, Key West, Florida.

We know our union is quick and unexpected, but when you've found your soul mate, there's nothing to do but take the plunge. We would love to have the pleasure of your company. RSVP to Jackie @ JackieBirchard@seaanemone.com.

Jeb's smile vanished. A muscle at his right eye jerked repeatedly. He had to read the text four times before the words finally sank in. Jackie was getting married on the Fourth of July. Six days from now. The precise number of days it would take *Second Chance* to sail from St. Michael's to Key West in calm waters.

And she'd invited him to the wedding via text message!

"A bit cowardly, Jackie," he murmured. "You could have had the decency to pick up the phone and call me."

He got to his feet, shoved his hands through his hair, paced and cussed a blue streak. How could she do this to him? She'd promised she would give him a year to prove he could change, and now she'd gone and gotten herself engaged to some guy in the Coast Guard? What the hell?

Jeb had to admit his feelings were hurt.

To top it off, she'd used the words *soul mate*. Jackie did not talk like that. She didn't believe in stuff like that. What had happened to her? She could not be thinking clearly. She must be caught up in some kind of lust-fueled haze, like the one he'd gotten ensnared in when he almost had sex with Haley on the beach. It happened. He understood. He could forgive her. What he couldn't do was let her make the biggest mistake of her life.

Distressed, he punched Jackie's number into the keypad.

She answered on the second ring with a cheery, "Hey, Jeb, long time no hear."

How could she sound so casual?

"I just got your text message," he said tersely.

"Will you be coming to the wedding? I know it's short notice, but it would mean a lot to me to have you there."

"Jackie, you can't marry this guy."

"Why does everyone keep saying that to me?"

"Who else said it to you?"

"Boone, for one." Boone was Jackie's half brother. "He was a bit of a jerk about it, too," Jackie continued. "At least I know you're not going to be a jerk. You're never a jerk about anything."

"Well, I'm with Boone on this one. You can't marry this guy."

"I can and I will. I'm in love, Jeb. For the first time in my life. Truly, madly, deeply, forever and ever in love."

"Okay, who are you and what have you done with Jackie Birchard?"

"I've changed, Jeb."

"I've changed, too, Jackie. I've changed so much and I miss you. You can't marry this Scott guy because I'm the man for you and I can show you if you just give me a chance."

"Jeb." She laughed. "You don't love me."

Laughed! She was laughing at him.

"But I do, Jackie, I really do."

"You think you love me because I'm the only woman who has ever turned you down. The only woman who's ever challenged you and called you on your crazy lifestyle."

Not the only woman. Immediately, Jeb thought of Haley.

"How long have you known this guy?" he demanded.

"Only a month, but the time doesn't matter. Not when it's the real deal."

"Listen to yourself. Do you really hear what you're saying? You're marrying a guy you've only know for four short weeks."

"It's all the time I need."

"Jackie, you've got to believe me—"

"Are you coming to the wedding?"

"I'm coming to Key West. Right now. I'm on my way. It'll take me six days to get there, winds willing. I'm on St. Michael's."

"You on the *Feelin' Nauti?*"

"I changed her name."

"Bad luck." Jackie hissed in a breath. She was a smart, educated woman working on her Ph.D. in oceanography, and yet, she had a sailor's innate superstition. It came naturally to those who spent their lives on the sea and understood that there were certain things beyond your control. Not breaking certain rules could make a sailor feel safer. It was psychological. They both knew it, but ingrained patterns of behavior were hard to break.

"It's not bad luck. I changed her name because of you."

"What are you calling her these days?"

"*Second Chance.*"

"Oh, Jeb."

"Promise me you won't get married until I get there."

"I can't promise that. The wedding is at four."

"Then I will find a way to be there before four."

"Good, should I put you down for fish or filet mignon?"

"What?" he asked, thrown off by the question.

"Fish or beef. For the reception head count."

"Once I get there, there won't be a reception."

"Oh, Jeb, you are so funny. I can't wait to see you again."

"Jackie, I'm being serious—"

"Gotta go, honey, another call is coming in. I've been nuts with the RSVPs. See you on Saturday, if not before."

The dial tone sounded in his ear.

Honey? Jackie had called him *honey?* As if he was some maiden aunt or the flower girl or something.

He thought about calling her back, but he realized no matter how hard he tried to tell her that he'd changed, she'd simply have to see it to believe it. Okay, he deserved that. He'd been fickle and shallow in the past, but his year on St. Michael's truly had transformed him. The only way that Jackie was going to know he was serious was if he showed up at the wedding, got down on bended knee and asked her to marry him instead of Scott.

After all, she'd only known Scott a month. How serious could it really be if she'd only known him a month? She and Jeb had known each other through nautical circles since they were kids. His family had helped finance many of Jack Birchard's research trips before he'd gotten as famous as Jacques Cousteau. That was how Jackie knew him so well. Even before they dated, she'd heard of all his exploits. That was the main strike against him. She'd witnessed his dating history firsthand.

There was only one thing to do. Sail to Key West immediately and confront Jackie face-to-face.

THE ROCKING MOTION was so nice, a gentle lullaby soothing Haley's splitting headache. Her eyes were closed and her thinking was fuzzy. She should open her eyes and see where she was, because she'd forgotten, but a provocative fragrance distracted her.

What was that enticing scent? It smelled like sea and cotton linen and masculine man.

Jeb.

It smelled like Jeb.

Mmm, Jeb.

Dreamily, in spite of the headache, her mind conjured up her favorite image of Jeb Whitcomb.

November.

It was last November on Divers' Beach at sunset.

After a taxing twelve-hour shift at what was then a makeshift tent hospital, Haley had decided to take a long walk to clear her head. She'd been working nonstop since she'd arrived with the Red Cross on St. Michael's the previous June and she was close to the breaking point. She just needed some alone time and Divers' Beach was the most secluded stretch of sand on St. Michael's. Especially since Hurricane Sylvia had driven many people to leave the island for good.

The beach had been cleaned up, but there were still

big piles of brush stacked up in the tree line awaiting disposal. Her heart ached for the damage her adopted home had suffered.

As a child, she'd spent her summers on the island. Her parents were teachers and each year they volunteered as instructors for a program to help disadvantaged children get the education they needed. It was a win-win situation. Free vacation for her and her sister and brother, while underprivileged children got the assistance they needed. The experience taught Haley the power of giving to others.

That was when she happened upon Jeb, who was up to his waist in the surf, the golden rays of the evening sun glinting off his bare chest. At first, she thought he was dangerously swimming alone—which was sort of what she might expect from a guy who liked to test limits, except he never went anywhere alone—and then she realized there was a flailing seagull in the water beside him.

Jeb approached and soothed the frantic bird, and then he plucked a plastic six-pack ring holder from around the gull's legs. Freed, the bird launched itself into the air. Jeb stood there watching it soar, a happy smile on his face, unaware he was being observed.

When he turned back around and spotted her, he looked chagrined for a fraction of a second, as if embarrassed to be caught saving a seagull's life, but then quickly he started preening, flexing his biceps and strutting like a badass, almost killing the tender scene she'd just witnessed.

He sauntered ashore, water rolling off his body, black swim trunks clinging to his hips. Haley gulped, noting they were completely alone on the beach.

"Hey," he greeted her, stuffing the plastic six-pack holder into the pocket of his swim trucks. "Fancy meeting you here."

The previous day, they'd had an argument at the meeting of the hospital planning committee. He wanted to put an open-air solarium in the middle of the new hospital. She thought the money would be better spent on more monitoring equipment. He'd won, of course. He was paying for the hospital, after all, but she did have to give him props for at least hearing her out, and then today, the administrator had told her that Jeb had cut an extra check to cover the equipment, too.

She was still in her hospital scrubs. She hadn't taken the time to change. Home at this point was still a communal tent in the town center.

"Thanks," she said, always able to admit when she was wrong about someone. "For buying the equipment."

"Thank *you*."

"What for?"

"Making sure that my priorities were straight. Notice that no one else on the committee protested my plans?"

"No one ever goes against you."

"Except for you." He'd grinned at her as if that was a good thing.

She found herself softening toward him, but that scared her because she was just as attracted to him as everyone else. She was *not* going to give in. She'd done the hero-worship thing before and that had turned out badly.

"Where's your entourage?" she asked.

"I gave 'em the slip." He winked conspiratorially.

She warmed from the inside out. "What for?"

"Sometimes a guy just wants to be alone."

"I'm shocked," she teased. "I never considered that you got tired of being adored."

"It's not all it's cracked up to be," he answered in a moment of honesty that took Haley by surprise.

"Well…" she said. Could it be more awkward between them? "I'll leave you to your privacy."

He put out a hand to touch her arm.

Her skin ignited. Like gasoline on a fire.

"Don't go," he said.

"I don't want to intrude."

"You're not." His smile was soft and inviting and she just swooned. "May I walk with you?'

She nodded and he fell into step beside her.

They walked along in silence for a while and then stopped to watch the sun slide down the horizon. It winked out, leaving a salting of stars in its wake.

"It's very peaceful," he said.

She took a deep breath, acutely aware of how close he was to her, how good he smelled and how kind he'd been to rescue that seagull. It was the only excuse she had for what happened next.

"Haley," he murmured and lowered his head. "You've bewitched me."

"What?" she squeaked.

"I can't seem to stop thinking about you."

"Me?"

"You."

"But why? I'm nothing special."

"You underestimate your beauty."

Yeah, right. Here she was with no makeup on, hair pulled back in a ponytail, wearing shapeless green hospital scrubs, and he was telling her she was beautiful. In a pig's eye. "I'm fully aware of my physical attributes. I have nice legs, I'll grant you that, and decent hair, but I'm no supermodel. I have a gap between my teeth and my eyes are just a little too wide set and my chin is too pointy—"

"All those things come together to create an interesting face. Do you know how deadly dull most supermodels are? After a while they all look alike. Be proud of your distinctive looks. You're an original."

"Oh," she said because she was embarrassed by his compliments. She wasn't accustomed to being buttered up and Jeb was slicker than olive oil. She could not forget that.

"But as pretty as you are, it's not your looks that intrigue me." He stepped closer.

"No?" She was barely breathing now.

"Nope."

She gulped.

"What I like most about you is your ethics."

"Yeah, that's so sexy. Guys tell me all the time I have gorgeous ethics."

"They do?"

"I'm being snarky."

"And your dry sense of humor. I like that, too, although I'm not sure I'm sharp enough to always get your jokes."

"You're being humble?" Haley put a hand to her forehead and pretended to faint.

"I like how grounded you are and how you set a good example for those around you."

"What's this all about, Whitcomb?" she asked suspiciously. "Why are you flattering me?"

"It's not flattery. I'm being sincere."

She eyed him speculatively.

"I know we butt heads and I want to smooth things out."

"Ah, you mean you want to convert me to your way of thinking."

"No," he said, "not at all. Didn't I mention that I like the way you challenge me? I just want to be clear that a little healthy disagreement is a welcome thing."

"I'll remind you of that the next time I disagree with you."

"Do that." He nodded vigorously.

She wasn't sure what to do. She'd never really seen this side of him. Of course, she'd never really been alone with him, either.

The water lapped at the shore, a whispering, seductive rhythm. The breeze ruffled the leaves of the palms and the air smelled of coconut. The moon started its ascent up the sky.

Jeb peered deeply into her eyes. His lips were so close, just inches away, and his chest was so bare, his skin so tanned and her knees so weak. Such enticing lips they were, angular and full, but not too full. What would his lips taste like? How would they feel against her mouth? What would they make her feel?

She got trapped in his eyes. Trying to snap out of it, she lowered her lashes and her gaze became tangled up in the stunning view of his muscled torso. Jeb was like a pirate ready to plunder a cargo ship weighted with gold. Within her personal space, his unique masculine scent claimed her.

"This is nice," he murmured. "Being here with you."

"Nice," she echoed.

"You know," he said, "if I didn't—"

But he never got to finish, because damn her, she'd just acted, which was something she never did—no one had ever accused her of being spontaneous—but in the moment, she went completely off the rails, flung her arms around his neck and kissed *him*.

Haley didn't know who was more surprised, her or Jeb.

For a second, he simply stood there not kissing her back and she'd thought, *What have I done?*

Then he groaned low in his throat, gathered her in his arms and pressed her to his chest. The chest she'd just been aching to touch. His abs were as taut and hard as she had imagined they would be.

He made a deep, pent-up sound as his lips assailed her, his tongue striking like heated lightning on a still, cloudless day. Her body was stunned, thrilled. He tugged gently on her ponytail, tilted her head back and thrust his tongue farther inside of her.

She clung to him.

Moaned. Pulled him down to the sand. The soft-packed damp earth was cool against her spine and he was astride her, his knees sunk into the sand. He stared down into her eyes with wonder and shock. He was hard and she was—oh, this was the shameful part—she was whimpering for more.

Her fingers plucked at the waistband of his shorts.

His eyes darkened.

Her heart thumped.

His hands were all over her, burning her up, building sweet pressure within her body. Construction. He was a builder and she was the structure he was erecting. His lips laved hers, a pleasing foundation, a solid beginning, the underpinnings.

He used small, quick kisses. And long, big, bold kisses that lasted for minutes. And at last, when she was certain that he couldn't possibly do more, he covered her mouth with a kiss of considerable duration. A kiss that sizzled with energy and, like a tower of blocks, stacked one atop the other, rising higher and taller, reaching for the stars, sweeping the top of the moon, climbed to dizzying heights that promised she'd never, ever feel anything like this again.

Just when she was about to rip off her clothes, bare herself to him and beg him to take her right there on the sand, Jeb had stood up and stepped away from her.

"I can't do this," he said hoarsely.

"Please," she begged. Yes, she'd begged. "You can't leave me like this."

"Haley—" he shook his head "—you deserve so much better."

He was turning her down?

Shame shot through her. She couldn't even interest a playboy? She jumped up, dusting off the seat of her scrubs.

"I don't mean to hurt you. Another time, another place and I'd be all over this, but there's someone else and—"

"Stuff it, Whitcomb," she'd growled to hide her deep humiliation.

"Haley." The pain in his voice sounded genuine, but she wasn't sticking around to find out. She'd run from him then, as fast as she could.

She shoved the memory out of her mind and her

eyes flew open. She stared up at the ceiling, and for a second, she was disturbed to see she wasn't in her bed.

Where was she?

It hit her. Bricks. Tons of them. Falling in on her. The party. Rick. The suspect salty dog. Staggering to the bathroom.

She'd spent the night in Jeb Whitcomb's bed! Fully dressed in Ahmaya's sexy Ann Taylor Loft spaghetti-strap dress and ridiculous stilettos. She had to get out of here.

Now.

She leaped off the mattress, landed wrong, staggered against the door. Strange, it felt as if the boat were moving—probably just the wake from a passing speedboat rocking the yacht in the marina slip. Except this motion felt a lot stronger than simple wake ripples.

It felt as if they were under way.

But they could not be under way. Jeb wouldn't leave the dock with her on board. Surely he knew that *someone* was on board. His bedroom door had been locked. He had to know she was in here. Bedroom doors did not lock themselves from the inside. Besides, hadn't Ahmaya come looking for her? Wasn't her friend concerned?

Alarmed, she unlocked the door and lumbered out into the hallway. No one was around, but the lower deck was as neat as a pin. Someone had cleaned up and she hadn't even heard it? How long had she been out? Luckily, today was her day off from work, but still, this was unsettling. Where was Jeb?

Slowly, she climbed the stairs to the next deck. "Hello?" she called out. "Jeb? Anybody?"

No answer.

With a sick feeling settling in the pit of her stomach and her head throbbing as if there were a miniature construction crew up there whacking down walls with a sledgehammer, she eased up the final set of stairs to the bridge and looked around.

She spied Jeb at the helm with his back to her, his whiskey-colored hair blowing in the breeze, a serious set to his shoulders.

Reality hit like the slap of a palm against her cheek. Not only were they under way, but it was also late afternoon, and there was nothing around as far as the eye could see except for miles and miles of turquoise ocean.

5

Sheet—*The line used to let out or trim in a sail*

"What are you doing?"

Startled, Jeb whipped around to see a woman standing behind him. The hairs on the nape of his neck lifted. What the heck?

It was Haley, her hair in a mad tangle, her dress rumpled, her eyes blazing sparks.

His stomach lurched. He was so stunned to see her there that all he could say was "I…I…um…uh…I…"

"Where are we? Where are we going? Why are we not in the marina? Why are you kidnapping me?" She spit out rapid-fire questions, her tone accusatory.

Flabbergasted, his jaw dropped. "Kidnapping you? Why are *you* stowing away on my boat?"

"I didn't stow away. It was not my intention to stow away. I am not a stowaway."

"And yet here you are." He engaged the autohelm so he could give her his full attention and turned to face her.

"You took off without my permission."

"Clearly, you spent the night aboard without *my* permission." He raked his gaze over her. How could he not have known she was on board? "Or without my knowledge."

"Turn this boat around and take me back to shore," she demanded.

"Excuse me?"

She raised her chin, indignant. "You heard me."

Jeb laughed.

"Stop laughing at me." She scowled. "This isn't the least bit funny."

"It's a little bit funny."

"Not from my perspective."

"Seriously, French, do you ever see the humor in a situation?"

She looked hurt then, but quickly blinked it away. "I was a bit rude earlier. Excuse me. It was just an eye-opener to wake up and discover I'm out to sea."

"Apology accepted."

"Now, please return me to shore."

Jeb shook his head. "Sorry, no can do."

She stepped closer. "Why not?"

"For one thing, we've been under way since dawn."

"What time is it now?"

"Three-fifteen p.m."

"Three fifteen! That means we've been gone—"

"Eight and a half hours."

The column of Haley's throat moved in a visible gulp. "You have to take me back."

"I don't like this situation any better than you do, but I can't." He was already wondering how this was going to look to Jackie, showing up at her wedding with another woman. He couldn't show up at the wedding with Haley. Once he'd cleared customs and immigrations in Key West, he'd stick her on a plane back to St. Michael's. Jackie would never know.

"What do you mean, you can't?"

"I have to get to Key West by Saturday. It's doable, but only if the winds and currents cooperate. If I take you back, I don't stand a chance. We have to crab the tempestuous Gulf Stream and that's always a crapshoot, although luckily, the weather report indicates smooth sailing."

"Crab?"

"In order to compensate for the Gulf Stream current, you have to sail a bit to the side of the actual course in order to reach it."

"I get it. Moving sideways like a crab."

"That's it."

She surprised him by plucking the sunglasses from the pocket of his shirt, her fingers lightly—accidentally—grazing over his nipple, and his body responded immediately.

Dammit!

She slid his sunglasses onto her face, and a surge of something dark and sexy moved through him.

"Go right ahead. Make yourself at home. What's mine is yours," he said.

"Do you mind? I have a headache, and since you did kidnap me—"

"Didn't kidnap you. Had no idea you were on board."

"Nonetheless, I'm out to sea against my will without my sunglasses."

"Too much wine last night?"

"Too much salty dog with some kind of drug in it."

"What?" Alarm rippled through him.

"Why else do you think I was passed out in your bedroom for sixteen hours? Alcohol alone wouldn't knock someone out that long."

"Cabin."

"What?"

"A bedroom on a boat is called a cabin."

She waved a hand. "Whatever. Anyway, I have a strong suspicion that creepy respiratory therapist Rick Armand spiked my salty dog with something."

Part of him wanted to say that if she hadn't tried to escape him by running off with Armand that it wouldn't have happened, but another, stronger part of him had a vivid image of grabbing Armand by the throat and shaking him until his eyes popped out of his head or his mustache fell off, whichever came first. "The creep drugged you?"

Massaging her temple, Haley told him what had happened to her the previous night.

"I'm truly sorry," he apologized, "that this happened to you at my party."

"It wasn't your fault. Rick is a sleazebag. I already suspected it, but now it's confirmed. I was going to make a report to the St. Michael's police, but by the time I get there the drug will long be out of my system and there's no way I can prove he did it. All I can do is warn the women at the hospital to be wary of him."

"I'd help you do it, too, if I were going back."

She grimaced. "So I *am* being kidnapped."

"Not kidnapped. Whisked away for a few days. Think of it as a vacation. When we get to Florida, I'll put you on a plane back to St. Michael's."

"In the meantime, I'm stuck with you."

"Is that so horrible?"

Her grin was tiny. "Could be worse, I suppose. I could be stuck out here with Rick the dick."

"Over my dead body," he said vehemently.

"So why are you crossing the Gulf Stream?"

"I have to stop a wedding."

For the first time since she'd come onto the bridge, she looked something besides distressed, upset or angry. Curiosity sparked in her eyes. "Whose wedding?"

"My ex-girlfriend is getting married to a guy that she's only known for a month."

"And you don't think she should marry him?"

"She should marry me," he declared.

"You?" Haley hooted as if it was the funniest thing she'd ever heard.

Annoyed, Jeb frowned. "Why do you find that so humorous?"

"Hey, five minutes ago you were accusing me of not having a sense of humor. I just never pictured you as the marrying kind."

Actually, neither had Jeb, but since Jackie had started him off on his personal journey, he really had started to change. Going to St. Michael's was the most monumental thing he'd ever done.

"So what's the story?" Haley sat down on the hammock and reached down to unbuckle the stilettos from around her gorgeous feet.

It did weird things to him to think about her sweet fanny sitting where he'd just been sleeping. It felt strangely intimate. Just as intimate as when he thought about her having spent the night in his bed, and dammit, he'd missed it.

Seriously, what was wrong with him? He was talking about marrying Jackie, and here Haley's delicious bare pink toes wriggling against the deck were turning him on. Maybe he hadn't changed as much as he'd thought.

Haley rocked gently in the hammock, swinging back and forth with mesmerizing motion.

Jackie, Jackie, Jackie, he chanted to remind himself of his goal. He was going to Key West to stop Jackie from marrying this Coast Guard Scott character.

Jeb tried to call up his former girlfriend's face, but to his complete shock, for one blind instant, he could not remember what Jackie looked like. When he tried, he couldn't picture anyone except for Haley. Alarmed, his mind raced through his mental cache of old girlfriends—Kellie, Ashley, Heather, Robin, Brenna, Jane, Erin, Sophia, Lucy, Emily, Rachel, Jackie.

Nada.

He couldn't call up any of them because the woman in front of him was absorbing every bit of his attention.

A leopard can't change its spots, Jackie had told him.

Jeb was determined to prove that wasn't true. He could settle down. More than that, he *wanted* to settle down. This was all a startling new development.

Haley put out a toe to the bench seat. "Have a seat and tell me about her."

"Who?"

"This woman you're crabbing the Gulf Stream for."

"You don't want to hear about her."

"Why not?"

"Why?"

"Because," Haley said, "this is the most real I've ever seen you. For once, instead of being a guy regularly idolized by adoring females, you're the one behind the eight ball."

"You're enjoying my misery, aren't you?"

She slanted her head, grinned and winked. "Not at all. I just enjoy getting a glimpse at the human being lurking behind the slick facade."

MAYBE IT WAS BECAUSE she was overwhelmed at finding herself all alone with Jeb Whitcomb in the middle of the ocean on his yacht with St. Michael's eight and half hours behind them. Maybe it was the lingering effect of being drugged and the dull headache that had settled behind her eyes. Or maybe it was the fact that what Jeb was doing was so romantic it disarmed her.

"Jackie's the reason that we…that you…that we didn't do it that night on the beach?" she asked.

"Yep."

"Well," she said, "that makes me feel a little better. I thought it was me."

"Oh, no, ma'am. Not you. Not by a long shot. In fact, your very sexiness is what had me turning tail and running. I was not going to fall back into old habits."

That should have cheered her up, but it didn't and she couldn't say why.

Aw, c'mon. You know the reason why. You're jealous of this Jackie woman.

He kept talking about her, which was annoying, particularly since Haley was the one who had encouraged the conversation in the first place. Then he told her that Jackie was the daughter of the world-renowned oceanographer Jack Birchard. But of course, Jeb was in love with someone of his own ilk…a rich celebrity type. It was stupid of her to think he might fall for a lowly nurse.

Holy Oreos.

Was that what she was secretly hoping? That Jeb would fall in love with her? Ashamed of herself, Haley pushed his sunglasses farther up on her nose, thankful that her eyes were hidden from him. She didn't want him seeing her thoughts written on her face.

She should get over herself and be happy for him. Well, except that the woman he was in love with apparently loved someone else. Wasn't that just the way of love? Fickle. Stupid. Love oughta be banned.

"So," he said, "I do appreciate your patience and understanding."

"I gotta call Ahmaya." She jumped up. "She's going to be freaking out."

"You might not be able to get cell-phone reception out here. We are pretty far from shore."

"I have to try." Where was her purse? Down in Jeb's cabin, no doubt. "I'll be right back," she said and hurried to the lower deck.

She found her purse on the floor of his bedroom, fished out her cell phone and put a call in to Ahmaya.

"Haley!" Ahmaya answered on the first ring. "You naughty girl."

"Naughty?"

"Spending the night with Jeb Whitcomb after you pretended not to like him. I knew you really had a crush on him."

"I did not spend the night with him."

"Your car was still in the marina parking lot when I left the yacht at two o'clock."

"Why didn't you come looking for me?"

"I did. You were nowhere to be found and now I know why."

Static crackled over the airwaves. "Ahmaya, I don't know how long the connection is going to last, so just listen to me."

Quickly, she explained the situation.

"That's awful!" Ahmaya said. "I knew that Rick couldn't be trusted."

"Anyway, will you tell the director of nurses I had an emergency situation?" That was true enough. "And I need to take a week of vacation."

"Okay. I'm sorry, Haley."

"What for?"

"You finally get to be all alone with Jeb and you find out he's got a thing for another woman. That's gotta hurt."

"I'm fine, really," she said, but her heart gave a strange little tug.

"Be—"

The phone cut out.

"Ahmaya? Are you there?"

Nothing.

"Ahmaya?"

Dead.

Well, at least she'd gotten through long enough to let Ahmaya know where she was. Sighing, Haley hung up. She'd just lost her last contact with the outside world. It felt monumentally scary to realize she was out on the open sea. Stuck in this skimpy party dress. For six days. With Jeb Whitcomb.

Six days.

And five *nights*.

Right. Too bad she couldn't stay down here in the cabin for the duration of the trip. Her stomach rumbled, reminding her of one major reason she couldn't stay down here. She hadn't eaten anything since the hors d'oeuvres the previous evening and she was starving.

As if by magic, she caught a whiff of something delicious. Bacon. Yum.

Drawn by the scent, she went to the galley.

Jeb stood at the stove frying up bacon through a brown haze. Oops. Not a brown haze. Brown lenses. She was still wearing his sunglasses. She slipped them off her face and she could see him clearly now. Far too clearly if the truth be told.

His feet were bare, showing off very sexy toes. Who knew toes could be sexy? His hair was windblown, his cheeks bronzed. He looked every inch the wealthy yachtsman.

"Did your call go through?"

"Just in the nick of time. I lost the signal, but Ahmaya's going to make my excuses to the director of nurses."

"I appreciate your being such a good sport about this, Haley, but I shouldn't be surprised," he said. "You're at your best when you're helping people."

"Hey, I'm simply along for the ride, reluctantly, I admit, but there's nothing to be done about it. I really can't expect you to spend over eight hours returning me to the island when you're on a mission to win back the woman of your dreams."

"Thanks for understanding." He pushed a tall glass

of iced tea toward her. "Drink. It's easy to get dehydrated on the water, and after what Armand pulled, you need to flush out your system."

"Thanks." She took the glass of tea. It was so refreshing and cool, she sucked down the whole thing in nothing flat.

"I thought you might be hungry, too." He flipped bacon.

"I could gnaw the arm off that chair."

"No need. I'm making BLTs. You do eat meat, don't you?"

"I try not to eat red meat too often, but I love it." Unable to resist the enticing aroma any longer, she reached over to filch a piece of bacon from the cooling rack. Crisp, crunchy, salty. Perfect. "May I help?"

"You can slice up a tomato." He pointed at the garden-ripe beefsteak tomatoes in the wicker basket on the table.

"I can't believe you know how to cook," she said, plucking a tomato knife from the Calphalon knife block resting on the granite countertop.

"Why's that?"

"I figure you grew up with cooks and servants at the ready to do your bidding."

"I did," he admitted. "But my mother believed her sons should know how to prepare a meal, so she got the cook to teach us."

"The cook?"

"We had live-in help."

"Smart mother. I like her style."

Jeb shot her a sideways glance. "She would like you, too. You're not an Airy."

"An Airy?"

"That's what she called my girlfriends. Airy, short for *airhead*. Except for Jackie. Jackie is the opposite of an airhead."

"Like me?"

"Like you," he echoed, his gaze warming her skin.

"So you date airheads for fun, but when you decide to get serious, you go in the other direction."

"I was never serious about Jackie until she dumped me. We've known each other since we were young and she was more a friend than anything else, but when she told me she had no interest in life with a playboy, well, I gotta admit that it hurt my feelings."

"I'm liking Jackie more and more."

"Because she hurt my feelings?"

"Because she pushed you in the right direction." This was such a bizarre conversation to be having with the man she was half hung up on. Okay. She was admitting it. She liked Jeb. Stupid time to find out. Or maybe she only liked him because she knew there was little danger of him liking her back now that he was hot to stop Jackie from marrying someone else.

"Honestly," he said, "I never thought Jackie would get married. She's so wrapped up in her work."

"Maybe that's why you were dating her in the first place." Haley washed two plump tomatoes in the sink, scrubbed the tender red skin. "Because she wasn't a threat to your bachelorhood."

"Then why do I want her back?"

"Because you can't have her. We always want most what we can't have."

He shifted his stance to look at her. "Do you really believe that?"

She shrugged. "It's a theory."

"I just know I have to see her."

"So," Haley said, desperate to talk about something else besides the love of his life, "how many brothers and sisters do you have?"

"Two half brothers and a half sister. Three stepsisters and a stepbrother."

"That's a lot."

"My parents—" he waved a hand "—have trouble staying married."

"No full siblings?"

"Nope."

"Where are you in the birth order?"

"My dad had a daughter when he married my mother. They had me and then got divorced. Dad remarried a woman with two daughters. My mother remarried a man with a son. Then my mother and her second husband had a son and daughter and my dad and his fourth wife—"

"Fourth?"

"It seems to have stuck this time. He and Pam had a son. My half-brother Benjamin is five."

"And your mother?"

"She and Chet have been married twenty years now, so that's working out, too."

"I'm dizzy just hearing about it. How do you keep up with everyone?"

"It's old hat to me." He shrugged.

"I bet Christmas at your house is wild."

"I got tons of presents. When parents feel guilty for not giving you enough attention, they tend to buy your love."

Poor guy. It sounded as if he'd been shuffled from

pillar to post and been bought off. No wonder he was a bit materialistic. "What does your dad do for a living?"

"Runs the family business."

"Which is?"

"Shipbuilding."

"You weren't interested in that?"

"I like building houses. It's nice creating homes for people."

"That sounds odd coming from a playboy bachelor."

"Construction is in my background, but I want to blaze my own trail. Besides," he said a bit sheepishly, "I mostly build vacation condos."

"Did you take a big hit when the housing bubble burst?" Haley concentrated on neatly slicing the tomatoes and tried to ignore how close they were standing to each other and how good it felt to be near him.

He nodded. "But I have a trust fund from my grandparents and it gives me flexibility to do other things."

"Like rebuilding St. Michael's."

"Yes."

"Which you wouldn't have done if Jackie hadn't dumped you."

He shrugged, looked chagrined. "Probably not."

"So Jackie did a lot for your personal growth."

"She did." He turned the gas burner off and blotted grease from the bacon with a paper towel. "What about you? Do you have any brothers or sisters?"

"One of each. Both younger."

A head of iceberg lettuce rested beside the sink. He picked it up, smacked the bottom against the counter and pulled the core from it. He tore the sturdy leaves with long, tanned fingers.

Giddy buoyancy bubbled up inside of her. She had no explanation for it. It was probably a residual effect of being drugged the night before.

"Tim is in the Peace Corps after getting his degree in sociology, and Phoebe is still in college studying green technologies."

"Sounds like you come from a family of helpers."

"I do," she said proudly. "My parents are teachers and every summer they take part in a teachers-without-borders program. When I was growing up, St. Michael's was where they volunteered. They've been married thirty years and are as much in love today as on their wedding day."

"That's great," he said, sounding slightly wistful. "I can't imagine what that's like."

He spread out the lettuce, which glistened with the water he'd rinsed the leaves in, on another paper towel. Then those long fingers were at the loaf of artisan sourdough bread, slicing through the brown crust to the soft white center. A delicious shiver skipped down her spine. Why did she find watching him make sandwiches so erotic?

"Could you get the mayo from the fridge?" he asked.

Happy to have an excuse to step away from him, she hurried to the compact refrigerator and retrieved the mayo. This was craziness. She couldn't allow their proximity to throw her.

She cracked open the fridge. A package of double-stuffed Oreos sat on the top shelf.

"Oreos," she exclaimed. "They're my favorite, and you keep them in the fridge, too!" She might be in love. Any guy who kept her favorite cookie in the refrigerator was a man after her own heart.

"Where else would you keep them?"

"Exactly." She grinned at him over the refrigerator door. "Ahmaya says I'm nuts for taking up fridge space with them, but cold Oreos are so good."

"The best."

"Do you break them apart, eat the filling out, then eat the cookie?"

"Is there any other way to eat Oreos?"

"I love the creamy center."

"Why do you think I get double-stuffed? Twice the creamy goodness."

"You know, Whitcomb, you might not be such a bad guy after all," she said.

His eyes twinkled. "If I had known we'd bond over cold Oreos, I would have gifted you with a refrigerator full of them months ago."

She ignored that statement and passed him the mayo. "Here you go."

Their knuckles brushed in the handoff and her stomach did a stupid flip-flop thing. Motion of the ocean. Boats rolled. Exactly. That was part of the problem. Being at sea set up a certain rhythm, sweet lulling, a dulling of one's internal warning system. Or at least that was what seemed to be happening in her case.

Jeb slathered mayo on the sourdough bread, topped it with the bacon, lettuce and slices of beefsteak tomatoes she'd cut up. "Simple, but elegant and delicious," he proclaimed and handed her a sandwich on a plate, took the second one for himself and she could have sworn he added in a soft mumble, "not unlike you."

"What?" she asked, her heart suddenly pounding.

"Up top for the view?"

She blinked. "Huh?"

"To eat," he clarified and she felt silly for thinking he'd said that simple-but-elegant-and-delicious comment about her.

She touched her temple. "Right now I feel too much like a vampire to go into the sunshine."

"Right. I forgot."

They sat at the table across from each other. Haley dug into her sandwich. It was so good and she was so hungry that she had to remind herself to slow down.

"I like watching you eat," he said.

Feeling self-conscious, she stopped chewing.

"You're not one of those girlie girls who pick at their food. You go at it with gusto."

"You talking about the airheads?"

"I am."

"Does Jackie eat with gusto?"

"Actually, no. Jackie's head is so wrapped up in her research that she doesn't even take time to enjoy the food she eats. She is usually reading oceanography books or studying nautical charts or writing a paper and would chew shoe leather if you stuck it in front of her for breakfast. But you," he said with admiration in his voice, "you enjoy every bite."

"It probably comes from being a nurse and having to grab meals when and where I can. I appreciate any food I can get."

"You're fun to cook for."

"It's fun to eat what you cook."

He grinned at her and leaned in closer. Even through the mouthwatering aroma of bacon, bread and tomatoes, his scent wafted over her, that clean sunshine smell that spelled *J.E.B.* She had a wayward urge to bury her nose against his neck and take a lingering whiff.

"Dessert?" he asked.

"If you're talking Oreos, yes." She grinned. "My one great temptation."

"The only one?" he drawled, strolling over to the refrigerator to retrieve the Oreos.

"The only one I'm admitting to," she said in a tone far sexier than she intended.

"Why, Haley French, are you flirting with me?" He returned to the table, opened the package of cookies.

She lowered her lashes, gave him an enigmatic smile. Hey, this was fun. No wonder Ahmaya was an outrageous flirt. She reached for a cookie, twisted it apart and scraped the filling with her teeth. From her peripheral vision, she saw Jeb do the same thing, his movements mirroring hers. "Mmm."

"It's odd—" his fingers twisted apart a second cookie, one hand moving clockwise, the other counterclockwise "—that we've worked together for almost a year but we hardly know anything personal about each other."

"What's the point of getting to know each other better? You're gone from St. Michael's and there's the whole Jackie thing."

He stared at her with expressive eyes, and it might have been her imagination, but he looked slightly hurt. "Didn't mean to step on your toes. I know I do that a lot. Just thought it might be nice to know more about each other. Never can tell when you'll need a friend."

"I'm sorry," she apologized. "I can be a little

prickly sometimes. Not the best defense mechanism in the world, I agree."

"You feel like you need a defense mechanism against me?" He sounded surprised.

"You have a way of taking over every room you walk into. It can make those of us who are less secure feel threatened."

"You?" His mouth dropped. "Insecure? You are the most capable, competent person I've ever met."

"In my job, okay, I know what I'm doing, but in social situations? Where small talk and charming repartee are de rigueur? Not so much."

"You do better than you think you do."

Flustered, she glanced away and mumbled, "That's kind of you to say, but untrue."

"So," he said, "what should we talk about?"

That was the sixty-four-thousand-dollar question since they had absolutely nothing in common. "You're the suave, debonair one here. You pick."

"How about hobbies? What do you do in your spare time?"

"I pretty much work all the time or volunteer."

"Do you like movies?"

She shrugged. "As much as the next person, I guess."

"Sports?"

"Doing or watching?"

"Either."

"Not fond of watching sports on TV, but in person on a balmy summer night, baseball isn't bad. I'd much rather participate in a sport than watch someone else having all the fun."

He propped his cheek in his palm and studied her

as if she were the most fascinating person on earth. He had a way of making her feel special that she found unnerving. "What sports do you participate in?"

"Nothing much these days, but I used to be a marathon runner."

"That's impressive. Built for the long haul, huh? How'd you pick up the sport?"

"I started running to get over—" She stopped. She wasn't going to get into that. It was too personal of a topic to discuss with him. She shook her head. "Never mind why I started. Running cleared my head."

"Why did you stop?"

"Hurricane Sylvia."

"The bitch," he teased. "I run."

"I know. I've seen you on the beach."

"And you've never been tempted to join me?"

Tempted? Oh, yeah. That was precisely why she had not joined him. "I always had too much to do."

"C'mere." He motioned to her with two fingers.

"Huh?" she asked. What was he up to?

"Lean forward."

She reared back.

He laughed. "You always do the opposite of what I want you to do."

"What is it?"

"You're very suspicious."

"Some guy drugged me last night. Don't you think I'm justified?"

"I'm sorry about that, Haley." His eyes darkened. "I'm so glad you were able to lock yourself in my cabin. If Armand had touched one hair on your head…"

He let the sentence stay unfinished, but the expression on his face said it all. He would have made sure Armand would have paid for his actions. Too bad Jeb hadn't been there to watch out for her when—

Nope. She was *not* going to think about that.

"Seriously, lean forward."

Nervously, she leaned in toward him and all her muscles tensed.

He extended his hand toward her face.

She jumped.

"Easy, there." The pad of his thumb whisked against her bottom lip. "You've got a tiny dollop of Oreo cream. All gone now."

She felt her face heat.

"Maybe someday you'll tell me," he said, wiping his hands on a napkin, then balling up the napkin and tossing it onto his empty plate.

"Tell you what?"

"Why you're so jumpy around me."

"Probably not," she said. "I won't ever see you again after Saturday."

"You know—" his gaze locked on hers "—I can't help but feel that's a terrible shame."

You and me both.

What was going on with her? She had to get this under control or she was not going to be able to survive six days—*and five nights*—alone with him on this sailboat.

How had she gotten herself into this fix? More importantly, how was she going to get out of it unscathed?

6

Preventer—*A line or other device used to prevent the boom from accidentally moving from one side to the other*

JEB SPENT A RESTLESS NIGHT in the hammock. He'd insisted that Haley take his cabin and she'd only marginally argued with him about it, but no matter how he tried to block it out, he kept thinking about her down there. How she might be curled up in the middle of his bed, wearing one of his T-shirts that he'd loaned her since she didn't have anything to sleep in.

Finally, he fell asleep around two o'clock in the morning, but even as he slumbered, Haley invaded his dreams. He kept seeing those pert high breasts of hers, dreamed of those long legs wrapped around his waist, inhaled the scent of her hair, which smelled faintly of strawberries. He'd sat up bathed in sweat. Tossed. Turned. Marinated.

He knew what this was. Haley was his last temptation, the final test to see if he could truly remain faithful to Jackie. Haley was the universe's way of making him prove he was worthy of Jackie. Why else had fate put her right here on his boat in the middle of the deep blue ocean?

Actually, it was quite poetic when he thought about it. This last challenge to prove that the play had gone out of the boy.

This was his second chance. Time to take a stand. He was a full-grown man and his future lay ahead of him. He was excited about it. The thought of commitment didn't scare him as it once had.

Comforted, he went back to sleep only to repeat the Haley dreams all over again.

This time, the changing wind woke him.

Jeb didn't need a weather vane to tell him which way the wind was blowing. He'd been riding the ocean for so long that he could feel the shift before it happened, that brief, silent pause before the change occurred.

Dawn heated the water's cool shimmer. The wind blew toward Florida at a sweet clip. Jeb grinned. Today, they would sail.

He got out his maps and charts and hurried down to the galley to make breakfast before they pulled up anchor. On his arrival, though, he found Haley standing at the stove in his T-shirt, drinking coffee while she scrambled eggs. Toast popped from the toaster.

"You're up," he said.

"Surprise. I thought I'd do the cooking today since you did it yesterday."

The hem of his T-shirt hit her midthigh. He didn't want to notice, but c'mon, how could he not? He was only human and her legs were fantastic.

"Excellent," he said. "We can get a jump start on

the morning. The wind is up and at our backs. We're sailing today and we'll make better time."

"That's thrilling." She buttered the toast.

He poured himself a cup of coffee and spread out the charts, checking his coordinates and seeing whether he needed to alter the headings so the boat "made good." Haley put a plate of eggs and toast in front of him and sat down across from him.

"That looks very complicated," she said.

"Sailing is a complex endeavor."

"But fascinating."

"You can never learn all there is to know about the sea. I discover something new every time I'm on the water."

"I'm fascinated by your fascination."

"Do you know anything about sailing?"

"Not in the least."

Jeb grinned, shook his head. "I have so much to teach you, Grasshopper."

Haley salted her eggs. "Um…I found a pink bikini in the bottom drawer of your dresser. I wasn't snooping, I promise. I was looking for a pair of socks. My feet get cold at night."

Somehow, he found that completely endearing.

"The bikini is my size, and since we're on the water, I was wondering if it might be okay to wear it."

Okay? For Haley to wear a bikini? That was like asking if it were okay to frame the *Mona Lisa*.

"Sure."

"I mean, I don't want to offend the woman it belongs to. Does it belong to Jackie?"

"Jackie? In pink? Not hardly." Jeb had no idea whose bikini it was, but he didn't want to tell Haley that it could belong to any number of women, so he told a little white lie. "It belongs to one of my sisters."

The happy smile on Haley's face told him the white lie was the right move. "You're sure she won't mind if I wear it? I washed out the dress I wore on board."

"No problem," he said hoarsely as a shiver went straight to his cock. This talk of women's clothing was stirring him, especially in relation to Haley. "Go ahead and change and I'll meet you up on deck." He finished his coffee. "It's time to get sailing."

Because I have to get to Jackie as fast as I can before I do something with Haley that I'll live to regret.

HALEY WAS EXCITED.

She stood in the cockpit, listening to Jeb explain the parts of the sailboat and what they were called. There was a lot to absorb. There was the mast—the vertical pole that supported the sails. It rose up in the center of the sailing yacht. There was a horizontal pole called the boom. It supported the bottom of the mainsail.

"What do you like most about sailing?" she asked.

"The playing field is constantly changing. No two days are alike."

"The playing field?"

"In other sports, the playing field is always the same—the baseball diamond, the basketball court, the football field—but in sailing the playing field is the wind and the water, Mother Nature at her finest. You can never control or predict her." His eyes tracked over Haley's face. "A bit like you."

Haley's cheeks heated at his appraisal.

"The boom swings from side to side as the boat turns," Jeb said, going back to the lesson. "So be careful not to get in the boom's way as it swings or you could end up in the ocean."

"So now I know what the saying 'lower the boom' means."

"This is the mainsail. You'll also hear it referred to as the main. A sail is nothing more than a big sheet that catches the wind to help move your boat faster through the water."

She wrung her hands. "Should I be taking notes?"

"You'll pick it up as you use it. *Second Chance* has a headsail. Smaller boats often don't."

"What's the headsail?"

"It's the sail here in front of the mast. There are different types of headsails. One type is a jib."

"Jib. Jeb. Easy to remember."

"This headsail is a spinnaker. You use it when sailing downwind. We'll be using it today since we're going with the wind."

"Got it."

"Now, each part of a sail has a name, too."

"Yipes. My brain is getting overloaded."

"You know medical terminology—nautical terms are a piece of cake compared to that."

"Easy for you to say. You cut your teeth on this lingo. But I'm ready. What are the parts of the sail?"

"The head is the top corner of the sail." He indicated the top.

"I bet that term gets teenage boys laughing."

"And some immature adult males, as well. The tack is the front bottom corner of the sail."

"Head, the top, just like it sounds. Tack, the front bottom. Got it."

"The clew is the back bottom corner of a sail. The foot—"

"Let me guess,' she interrupted. "It's the bottom of the sail."

He grinned at her. "I knew you were bright. The leech is the back edge of the sail and the luff is the front edge."

"I thought you said the luff was like a brake."

"*Luff* has multiple meanings. When used as a noun, *luff* refers to the forward edge of a sail. When *luff* is used as a verb, it refers to the flapping motion a sail-cloth makes when it's undertrimmed. *Luff* can also be used as an adjective. As in luffing sails can't generate any power.

"And these are the battens." He showed her the solid slats that were inserted into pockets along a sail's leech in order to help the sail maintain its shape.

"I think I've got it."

"Don't forget the lines."

"Lines?"

"Ropes with a specific purpose."

"This is starting to sound like a bondage film," she teased.

His grin turned wicked. "And what would you know about that?"

"Just because I work all the time doesn't mean I don't know what goes on in the world."

"Hmm." He sent a look over her that had Haley flushing.

"The ropes," she prompted and then cringed because it sounded as if she was too eager to know more about ropes.

"The ropes." The way he said it sounded so seductive. "The Cunningham is the control-line system near the tack of the sail used to adjust the luff tension."

The word *tension* hung in the air, a taut line between them.

"I'm guessing that's so you can tighten or loosen the sail. Speed it up or slow it down?"

"Something like that." He lowered his eyelids to half-mast. "This is the halyard." He tugged on the thick rope that ran up the mast. "It's used to pull up the sail. You'll be doing that in just a minute."

"Me?"

"You."

"All by myself?"

"All by yourself."

"What if I mess it up?"

"We start over.

"This rope that's mounted on the boom—" he touched it "—is called the outhaul and it's used to control tension on the foot of the mainsail."

"You need ten hands to be a sailor."

"Doesn't hurt." He went on to tell her the names of the remaining ropes and what they did, and then he introduced the equipment that adjusted the ropes, including the block, the clear and the winch. By the time he was done, she was thoroughly confused.

"Whew," she said. "I'm so not ready for a pop quiz."

"But you now know enough to hoist the mainsail."

"I do?"

"Yep."

"I'm glad one of us is confident in my abilities."

"The first thing you do when preparing the mainsail is to insert the battens, which I've already done.

Then you attach the tack. C'mere and I'll show you how." He motioned to her and she stepped over.

"It's starting to sound like learning the human skeleton. The hip bone is connected to the thigh bone…"

"An apt analogy," he said. "Now we attach the clew with a shackle and then we feed the luff."

"Ropes, shackles, feeding the luff, this is a very kinky sport." Oh, wow, why had she said that? She was officially babbling. He was going to think she was flirting with him. She wasn't flirting with him.

Was she?

Stop it. Just stop saying anything remotely suggestive.

He simply chuckled and continued with his instructions. Once everything was harnessed and in place, they double-checked the sails. "Okay," he said, "I'm going to steer us into the wind and then we'll hoist the mainsail."

"I'm nervous. What if I ruin something? This is a very expensive boat."

"I'm right here to help you. You're brave as hell, Haley French. I've seen you in action. Compared to heading up a hurricane refugee camp, sailing is a piece of cake."

Once he had the boat in position, he guided her over to the winch and slipped his arms on either side of her waist to show her how to wrap the halyard line in a clockwise direction around the winch drum.

"Just enough times so you can hold the line without it slipping, but as the sail goes up, you'll need to add another wraparound or two," he explained.

His breath was warm on her ear. It tickled and she

almost giggled but managed to bite back the giddy sound.

"Now what?" she asked, resisting the urge to lean back against him just so she could feel his muscled chest against her spine.

"You get to jump."

"Off the board?"

"Nope, on the halyard line. Remember what the halyard line does?"

"Raises the sail."

He chucked her under the chin gently. "Good job."

"Tell me what to do."

"Stand at the mast where the halyard is just above your head."

"Let me guess, I jump up to yank the halyard downward."

"Exactly. I'll be in the cockpit taking up the slack in the line by pulling on the rope that's wrapped around the winch."

"I think I'm beginning to see how this works."

"When the sail reaches the top, the load will increase so that jumping will no longer be effective. At that point I'll grind the winch until the sail is at the top."

"Ooh," she said, "there you go with the dirty words again."

Holy Oreos, French. Will you stop with the flirting? The man is hung up on another woman. Just shut your gob already.

What was really disconcerting was the fact that she never acted like this. Ever. What was it about Jeb that turned her into a silly schoolgirl? She was acting like an eleven-year-old backstage at a Justin Bieber concert.

"Ready?" Jeb asked.

"Ready," Haley confirmed.

"Pull the halyard."

She jumped for the halyard line, grabbed it and started tugging. Jeb had moved to the cockpit, taking up the slack. As they worked together, the mainsail began to rise.

The sail flapped gaily. She was so relieved. This was fun. She suppressed the urge to do a little jig. But halfway to the top of the mast, the halyard hung up and no matter how hard she pulled, she could not get it to budge.

"Er, Jeb," she called over to him. "I think I goofed up."

"The luff is jammed. Common occurrence. Best way for you to learn. Just stop pulling on the halyard and I'll show you how to clear the jam." He crooked an index finger for her to come over to where he was standing.

The second she was within touching distance of him, every nerve ending in her body tingled and sang. *Really, Haley? This is getting pathetic.*

They got the sail back on track and Haley got her body under control, sort of. They pulled and tugged, winched and ground until the mainsail reached the top of the mast and it filled with wind. Once it was fully hoisted, Jeb showed her how to secure the halyard with the jammer and they moved on to the spinnaker.

Once the sails were hoisted, she and Jeb cleaned up the spaghetti of rope lying about the deck. When it was over, she was perspiring and a little breathless from all the unusual exertion.

Jeb took up his place at the helm and Haley was free to take a seat and enjoy the fruits of their labor, and oh, my goodness, it was exhilarating. She never expected sailing to feel so freeing.

Her hair blew across her face with the wind at their backs, her bare feet rested on the slick, polished fiberglass, the sound of the sails flapping and the rigging clanging against the mast, the beer that Jeb had passed to her cool in her hand.

It was so peaceful. The water was so utterly blue, the sun so shimmery bright it bleached everything it touched. She took a sip of the beer and it slid back sweetly bitter on her tongue. Her gaze gathered the horizon. A few cheerful white clouds played tag across the sky, and in the distance, she saw something and her heart leaped with joy.

"Dolphins!" she cried. "Jeb, it's a school of dolphins and they're swimming right along with us."

"They're curious creatures and they'll often follow boats."

"But we're going so fast and they're catching up to us! It's like they're playing chase." Her heart was thumping as she hung over the side of the boat, the dolphins overtaking them. "They've got spots on them."

"Atlantic Spotted Dolphins."

She glanced over her shoulder at him. "Not a very unique name."

"Jackie would call them *Stenella frontalis*."

There it was. The reminder of the reason Jeb was making this journey. A bit of joy leaked out of the moment. *Good grief, Haley. Knock it off.*

She turned her gaze back to the dolphins. The lead dolphin was almost beside her. He was close to eight feet long and was speckled with swirls of white spots all over his body. A polka-dot dolphin. She laughed.

"They're not born with spots, but get them as they age. Sort of like the reverse of fawns. By the time they're old, they're covered in spots."

She rested her chin on her arm, stared out at the blue sea and the gray speckled dolphins, and a sense of utter happiness closed over her. She shut her eyes for a moment, savoring the feeling so she could pull out the memory later when she needed cheering up.

When she opened her eyes again, the exuberant dolphins were in a free-for-all around the ship. Like synchronized swimmers, they leaped and spun, somersaulted and cartwheeled. What graceful athletes. What gregarious creatures.

Their zestful sense of play reminded her of someone else she knew.

Haley peeked another glance over at Jeb.

The wind tousled his hair. His hands were on the wheel. His grin was wide and toothy, his blue eyes crinkling at the corners. Wow, he was so gorgeous.

Her heart did an aerial pirouette, rivaling the dolphins' acrobatics.

Back again she went to the dolphins, torn between the beauty of the sea and the handsome man at the wheel.

The lead dolphin made eye contact with her, barked an adorable noise that she could hear above the rush of the wind, his mouth stretched in a grin as compelling as Jeb's. As if he were saying, "Come play."

The creature seemed so self-aware, as if something

special was going on inside its head. She was awe-struck, humbled and grateful. So grateful that fate had put her on this boat to have this beautiful experi-ence. It was worth the anxiety of being an accidental stowaway, fully made up for being drugged by Rick Armand.

She'd never felt so connected to the sea, to the earth, to the tides, to the sky. She was part of nature, not just moving through it or reacting against it. The rhythm of the ocean was within her. She felt a part of it in a way she'd never experienced before and it was a deeply moving moment.

Jeb chuckled. "It's fun to see you get so excited over something as simple as dolphins."

"It might be simple to you," she said, "but to me, it's miraculous."

"I know you've seen dolphins before around St. Michael's."

"Yes, but I've never been so close. I've never looked a dolphin in the eye and felt—"

"Connected," he finished for her.

Ah, he understood.

She was such a latecomer to the party. How had she not realized how incredibly special these wild crea-tures were? How strongly they could affect you. Im-mediately, she felt sorry for all the people on the land. For everyone who never got to experience this liber-ating high.

A dolphin from the middle of the pack pulled closer to the sailboat. So close that if Haley leaned over she could reach out and touch the dolphin's smooth, wet spotted back. The dolphin went down under the water, and when it appeared again, there was a sleek little surprise swimming under the scoop of its body. She was a mother!

"Oh, look, there's a baby!" Rapturously, Haley leaped to her feet.

"Haley! Be careful," Jeb called out.

She spun around to see what he was cautioning her about.

It all seemed to happen in slow motion.

The boom swung around and came right toward her, but her landlubber brain could not process the danger fast enough. By the time her muscles coiled to jump, it was too late. The boom clipped her in the midsection, knocking her to the floor of the boat.

Ooph!

All the air rushed from her body and Haley lay gasping like a guppy, staring up at the clear blue sky. Her ears rang and her stomach quivered.

Then a face blotted out the sky and the only thing she could see was Jeb, his brow knitted in a concerned frown.

"Haley, are you all right?"

She tried to nod, but since she couldn't yet breathe, the effort was moot.

His arms were around her, warm and comforting, and he was dragging her to safety out of the way of the boom.

"It's okay," he murmured. "You're going to be all right."

She was a nurse. She knew that. The wind had been knocked out of her, nothing more, but it was a helpless feeling, not being able to draw in air. An edgy panic hovered, waiting to attack.

Jeb crouched beside her, rubbed her back with an open palm. "Easy, easy."

The crisp cottony scent of his shirt mingled with the smell of sun and ocean and got tangled up in her nose. His chest was directly to her right. All she had to do was turn her head and her face would be buried against his chest.

She was so unnerved by the urge that she couldn't think. Couldn't speak. Still couldn't manage to breathe more than two thready, inconsequential inhalations.

"Haley." He sank down on his knees, positioning his murmuring mouth at the level of her ear. His hand felt so good at her back.

Without fully knowing why, she did turn toward him. His mouth was beside her lips now.

Almost touching.

"Jeb," she whispered and that was all it took.

His mouth was on hers, delicious as salted caramel. She knew that just like the moment with the dolphins, this was an experience she would never forget: the sound of the billowy sails flap-flap-flapping in the Atlantic breeze; the summer sun beaming down bright and hot, shining a million tiny fractured lanterns over the choppy caps of blue water; the smell of briny ocean spray; this handsome man, hard with muscles and pecan-colored hair, kissing a practical woman who'd forgotten what it was like to have fun.

Haley stored this memory in the vault of her mental photo album and swore to pull it out from time to time when she needed a reminder of how utterly sweet life could be.

Jeb had a knowing mouth. It had been places. Tasted many sophisticated things. Kissed many things:

the small of a woman's back, the nape of a neck, ear-lobes. She wanted him to explore all those places on her, but although hope perched like a bird on her shoulder, she knew the bird could never fly.

Not with this man. His heart belonged to another.

She should break off the kiss. She knew it. Her brain was yelling at her, *Do something! Anything! Just stop kissing him!*

But she did none of those things.

Instead, she twined her arms around his neck and pulled him down on top of her.

Who was she? What was she doing? She felt as if she were channeling some spritely mermaid turning the tables on a handsome fisherman by catching him in her net. Oddly thrilling, that image.

The taste of him nested in her head, created a home there. Fizzy champagne and chocolate-covered straw-berries and buttered lobster and caviar. Not that she'd ever eaten caviar, but he tasted how she thought cav-iar might taste.

You are in such trouble, whimpered her brain.

Butt out, retorted her body.

His lips sapped her energy, drained her free will like the receding tide pulling away from the shore, leaving boulders jutting up from the shoals, expos-ing things better left hidden, like seaweed and broken seashells and man-made refuse. Leaving her raw and vulnerable and helpless to resist his touch.

The kiss was a thrill beyond thrills. She felt ripe and achy and ready to be plucked. Rationally, she did not want this but she hungered for it. Hungered for him.

She tilted back her head, clung to his neck with the

curve of one arm. He took the kiss deep, his tongue sliding in to do blissful damage to her self-control. Their tongues were completely bonded as she took up the play and gave back as good as she got.

A sound welled up from deep in his throat, vibrated through him and into her, and Haley lit up. She'd delighted him!

Before her normal rational common sense could rally, before she planted her palms against his chest and pushed him away, before her sense of shame roused from having been anesthetized by Jeb's perfect mouth and energetic tongue, Haley lapped up every bit of his attention, reveling in the exquisiteness she would never experience again.

It was brilliant.

Then, as all brilliant moments must, it collapsed.

Jeb moved away, muttered an apology, cursed softly under his breath and left a frozen slab of emptiness icing up her heart.

7

Lifeline—*A line or wire all around the boat, held up with stanchions, to prevent falling overboard*

FOR THE REMAINDER of the day, Haley avoided him.

Jeb couldn't fault her. He'd behaved abominably. He'd tried so hard to be good, to resist the temptations of her gorgeous body in that tiny little pink bikini. Maybe Jackie had been right all along. Maybe he *was* incapable of commitment.

That saddened him.

He really did want to change, but was redemption beyond his control? Would pleasures of the flesh always woo him? Would he ever master his body? How could he prove to Jackie that he'd changed when he couldn't even prove it to himself?

Disheartened, he'd stayed at the helm until dusk. Haley had disappeared belowdecks after he'd kissed her, mumbling something about the sun having given her a headache. He knew the sun wasn't the source of her pain, but rather, his inexcusable behavior.

He sailed until night dropped around them like

a curtain and the smell of onions, garlic and cumin wafted up from the lower deck. His stomach grumbled and he realized he hadn't eaten anything since the scrambled eggs and toast that Haley had prepared for him that morning.

He'd just dropped anchor and lowered the sails when she appeared on the deck, moonlight shining off her guileless face.

"Dinner's ready," she said.

"You didn't have to make dinner."

"I needed a job to do." She'd put his T-shirt on over the bikini—thankfully. Her feet were bare and she used the toes of her right foot to scratch the calf of her left leg. It was a simple gesture and shouldn't have been at all sexy, but dammit, it was. "I'm not an idle person."

"I can eat up here if you like."

A slight smile flitted across her mouth. "Putting yourself in the doghouse?"

"I deserve to be there."

"Cut yourself some slack," she said. "You're only human."

That surprised him. "You're not mad at me?"

She shrugged. "Look, it happened in a split second of weakness. I'm as much to blame as you are, but we can get past this. You're in love with Jackie and I'm just along for the ride. It was never my intention to get in your way. We've got a few more days alone out here together, so let's not make a bigger deal of this than it is."

Her attitude was a relief. She didn't hold the kiss against him. Of course, he couldn't let himself off the hook so easily, but her acceptance took some of the tension out of the air.

"I made tacos. C'mon, if you're coming." She turned and went back belowdecks.

Jeb took off after her.

A moment of awkwardness settled over them, as it always seemed to do when they sat down to eat together. Down here, the confines were close and there were no other distractions. They had only each other for company.

"Your cheeks are a little red," he said. "Sunburn and windburn can leave you feeling sore. There's some aloe-vera gel in the medicine cabinet."

"Thanks, I'll put some on before I go to bed." Her long, slender fingers picked up a taco and she tilted her head to eat it.

Another awkward pause.

Think of something neutral to say.

"So," he said, "how long are you planning on staying in St. Michael's?"

She swallowed her bite of taco, patted her mouth— that sweet pink mouth—with a napkin. "I'm not sure."

"Where will you go after that?"

"I'm thinking about becoming a traveling nurse. My time on St. Michael's has stirred up a wanderlust I never knew I had."

"Funny." He lifted his eyebrows.

"What?"

"Just when I'm itching to settle down, you're looking to roam."

"Ironic, I suppose. The stick-in-the-mud turns adventurer and the adventurer is looking to get stuck in the mud."

"Well, I've got to say, you're one heck of a sailor."

"You can say that with a straight face after I got hit by the boom? And after you warned me about it, too."

"You haven't gotten seasick. The majority of people get seasick."

"I've never had motion sickness in my life. Cast-iron stomach." Haley patted her belly.

Helplessly, Jeb found his gaze drawn to her flat midriff. She had such a narrow waist and such nice curvy hips. He could see the outline of the pink bikini beneath his white T-shirt.

It was official. She *was* killing him. Resolutely, he turned his attention to the tacos.

Sexy, gorgeous and a good cook, too? "Why hasn't some guy already snapped you up?"

"Pardon?"

Uh. Had he said that out loud? "There's no ring on your finger and you've never said anything about a boyfriend. Do you have a boyfriend?"

"No boyfriend."

"Why not?"

"My reason for coming to St. Michael's was to help people. How effective could I be if I was off dating when I should be working?"

"Everyone needs a break now and then."

'I'm beginning to see that," she said. "Today with the dolphins, well, it was the most fun I've had in a very long time."

Thinking about the dolphins led to thinking about what happened afterward and they both lapsed into silence.

"Plus," she said, "I didn't want to start anything I couldn't finish."

"So there's someone on St. Michael's you have your eye on?" he asked, feeling an irrational surge of jealousy.

She looked him in the eyes. "It was a passing fantasy."

"Do you always finish everything that you start?"

"I'm guessing you don't?"

"Not everything needs to be finished. Some things are meant to be temporary."

"Like a meal."

"Or a spontaneous riff."

"What's a spontaneous riff?"

"I'll do one with your name."

"Do what?"

"Riff."

"Okay, go."

"First, do you have any nicknames?"

She wrinkled her nose. "I'm not a nickname kind of girl."

"Someone in your life has called you by a nickname. Mother, grandmother, best friend, siblings."

"My friends call me Hale, sometimes. And my grandmother called me Pole Bean because I grew faster than the cousins. My dad occasionally calls me Haystack."

"Haley. *H* as in home and hearth. Only one *y*, not two. Tidy. Efficient. Hayley Mills, Halley's Comet. Haley. So dubbed by Mr. and Mrs. French. Hay. Haystack. Pole Bean. Grew tall and fast. Fresh. Clean-scrubbed. Dependable. Haley. Five letters. Two vowels tucked between three consonants. Evenly spaced. Steady, but with that surprising curly *y* at the end," he spit out in rapid-fire succession. "Haley. Beach beauty.

Golden skin. Slightly sad smile. Knowing eyes. Dimpled chin. Legs like a Thoroughbred. Dolphin lover. Crusader. Stiff upper lip. Scrupulous. Noble. Makes the best kick-ass tacos in the world."

She rolled her eyes. "Let me guess, this name riffing thing is a line, right? That you use on your dates?"

Honestly, no, he did not. He'd never used it. In fact, he had no idea where it had come from. The riff had just spun glibly off his tongue, but he was suddenly terrified to admit that to her. Then he realized he'd subconsciously been riffing her name for days, maybe even weeks.

"You can stop trying to charm me. I know it's second nature to you, but there's no point. So just relax."

She was right, there was no point, but in the back of his mind, a quiet voice kept on riffing—*Haley. Nourishing as wheat. Hospital tent. Slept on my sheets. Hard worker. Rubber-soled shoes. She's no shirker. Strawberry-scented hair that should never be pulled into a bun. Eyelashes like paintbrushes. Scared now and wants to run. Heart of gold. Puts me in my place like no one ever has. Turns Mr. Slick into Mr. Lacking Confidence. Haley. Came along for an accidental ride. Righteous lips. What do you want that I can't provide?*

"There's no charming you, huh?"

"Nope."

Another awkward silence.

"With the wind at our backs, we made really good time today," he said, rushing to fill the silence. "At this rate, we'll be in Key West on Friday."

She looked relieved. "That's good, and then we can both get back to our lives."

"Yes." But it didn't feel good.

Not good at all.

JEB RIFFING HER NAME had gotten to her.

Haley didn't want to admit it, but there it was. When Jeb had said all those nice things about her, she'd found a place for him in her heart. It was corny and she just knew he trotted it out for any woman caught in his orbit, but it was endearing. Goofy, but endearing.

Dinner was over. The dishes were washed—by them, together, and that had been wonderful and awkward as they'd bumped elbows. Now Jeb had gone up to his hammock on the bridge and Haley was standing in the bathroom brushing her teeth with one of the new toothbrushes Jeb kept stocked. But of course. He was the consummate host. Accustomed to having women spending the night on his yacht.

She stared at herself in the mirror, toothbrush poking out of one side of her mouth as she vigorously scrubbed her gums.

You're falling for him.

Haley shook her head, spat and rinsed. No. She wasn't falling for him. She was just, well, she liked him.

Uh-huh, tell yourself another lie.

Okay, so what if she was falling for him? Nothing could come of it for so many reasons, primary of which was the fact that he was sailing to Key West to break up an ex-girlfriend's impending marriage.

Her heart settled south of her stomach.

How she wished she could get off this boat and go back to St. Michael's. Back to her sane, normal life

filled with patients to take care of and away from beguiling ocean waves, captivating dolphins and Jeb
Whitcomb's super-sexy grin.

An overwhelming sadness washed over her. She'd
never felt so cut off. It was just her and Jeb. She
couldn't even call her friends or family for advice.
How was she going to survive the next few days with
him? Wanting him, yearning for him, but unable to
have him because he wanted someone else.

A tight band of misery constricted her heart. What
was wrong with her? Why did she feel so wounded
when she had no right to feel this way? None what-
soever.

She fingered her lips.

He might want another woman, but he'd kissed *her.*

*Only because you were convenient. Don't think it's
anything more than that.*

She was well aware of that, but there was this stupid red flag of hope jutting up in the back of her mind.
Anything was possible. Right?

Well, not this. A match between her and Jeb was
impossible for more reasons than his desire for Jackie
Birchard. He was wealthy and she was middle-class.
He loved to play and she was dedicated to work. He
was gorgeous and had women falling at his feet, while
she was of middling good looks at best. She could
not compete with the models and starlets and social-
ites who regularly vied for his attention, nor did she
want to.

Just get through the next few days. That was all
she had to do.

Yeah, as if that was going to be easy. Unless she

wanted to stay in the cabin for the remainder of the trip, there was no getting away from him.

Melancholia twined around Haley's stomach, insidious as seaweed. Was she going to stand here whining and feeling sorry for herself or was she going to do something about it?

Her pulse quickened at the idea of doing something about it. *Don't think. Just act.* Thinking was what had held her back for so long.

Barefoot, she leaped over the bed, grabbed for the cabin door, wrenched it open and sprinted the length of the lower deck to the stairs. Her hand touched the cool rail, stopping her instantly.

Her feet froze on the bottom step.

What was she doing?

What did she think was going to happen when she got up there on the bridge? That they would make wild, passionate love in the hammock? And what if they did? What then? He'd sail off into the sunset with Jackie and she'd be left feeling all hurt and sorry for herself because she'd followed an urge that led nowhere.

Why did it have to lead anywhere? Why couldn't she just have a good time? Was there anything wrong with that? What was it that Jeb had said at dinner? *Not everything needs to be finished. Some things are meant to be temporary.*

No. She would not be the razor Jeb used to cut himself. He was trying to prove he was no longer a glib playboy. He was trying to settle down. She could not be the temptation that crumbled him.

Slowly, she backed away from the stairs.

Go to bed. Start fresh tomorrow. Think about it tomorrow.

Yeah, Scarlett O'Hara, tomorrow is another day.

But for now, the night stretched out long and endless, and dawn seemed a hundred light-years away.

MIDNIGHT AND JEB was wide-awake.

Again.

Normally, he had absolutely no trouble sleeping. Especially when he was at sea; the gentle ocean rocking always calmed him. But tonight, things were even worse than they'd been last night because he'd kissed Haley.

Since he couldn't sleep, maybe he should get up and sail. Sailing through the night would put them that much closer to Key West. That much closer to getting Haley off his boat and on her way. But the accommodating winds that had swept them ahead of schedule today had also rolled in a batch of thick clouds. Tonight, the moon was obscured, peeping out only occasionally, and the air smelled of rain. Did he really want to risk getting caught sailing in a storm?

Better not push his luck. With today's progress, even if they experienced unexpected delays, he would easily make it to Key West before Jackie's 4:00 p.m. wedding on Saturday.

To get his mind off everything, he started going over the coordinates. He loved mental math. Longitude, latitude, changes in altitude. Hell, suddenly he was humming Jimmy Buffett.

Better than thinking about Haley.

Except now there she was again, lodged in his brain.

Argh!

He tossed off the lap blanket he'd been using, jumped to his feet, the hammock swinging wildly in his wake. He paced the deck, listening to the noises of his boat—the creak of the rigging, the whisper of water lapping at the hull, the hammer of his pulse in his ears.

Jeb walked toward the lower deck, climbed down the stairs. Stopped. Cursed himself. Climbed the stairs again.

Wait a minute. Was that a light he'd seen underneath the door of his cabin? Was Haley awake? He turned again, went back down.

Yep. A light.

Was she still up? Or did she sleep with a light on? Was she scared of the dark?

The urge to comfort her eclipsed him. Compelled by a force he couldn't seem to resist, Jeb crept closer.

He reached the cabin. Raised a fist to knock on the door, his breathing coming hot and fast.

Lowering his fist, he rested his ear against the door, imagined he could hear her breathing on the other side.

Haley.

His hand slid to the door handle. His entire body strummed and throbbed, each nerve cell tingling with an immediate energy that left his head reeling.

Haley.

What if she had her head against her side of the door? What if her heart was thudding as crazily as his?

And what if it wasn't?

He pressed his lips to the door, silently whispered her name.

Haley.

What the hell was he doing? He ground his teeth, spun around, raced on the balls of his feet—so he'd be quieter and she'd be less likely to hear him and come out—back to the haven of his hammock.

He swung the hammock madly, placed a palm to his forehead, gulped in air, remembered kissing Haley, hardened. Jerk. What the hell was the matter with him? He wasn't *that* guy. Not anymore. He was done with living in the moment at the sacrifice of the future. There were benefits to controlling yourself, to self-denial, to foregoing self-indulgence for the bigger picture, greater good, yada fricking yada.

Keep your fantasies to yourself, Whitcomb. Hands to yourself.

A year was such a damn long time to go without the feel of a woman's body beneath his.

Remember why you decided to stay celibate.

Haley.

What the hell? No, not Haley. Scratch that. Messed up on the name. Jackie.

Jackie, Jackie, Jackie. She was the one he wanted.

Ahem, Jackie is the one who is on the verge of marrying another man. She ain't busy pining for you. Yeah, well, that was why he had to get to Key West ASAP to correct his past mistakes.

Redemption. That was his goal.

Well, he wasn't going to get it by chasing after Haley.

Right. Yes. He knew that. He was on lockdown. *Don't dare get out of this hammock until dawn. No matter what. Got it?*

Overhead, yellow lightning flashed. Thunder rumbled. Even the weather was warning him.

Got it. He saluted the sky. He was all wet.

A few minutes later, soft sprinkles hit the deck, dropped lightly onto his face. He pulled the lap blanket up over his head.

The wind gusted, sent the hammock swaying. Goose bumps raised on his arms. He burrowed his butt in the hammock. If only the blanket were thick and woolen.

Lightning, now vivid blue, forked from the clouds, a jagged, electric snake tongue of illumination. Thunder clashed as loudly as a car crash.

Jeb jumped.

The rain sped up, pelting him.

This was not the safest place in a storm, but he'd checked the forecast. The storm should be short-lived and pass quickly with the blowing wind.

Except the wind seemed to have stalled, leaving the black clouds directly overhead, drenching him. Jeb flopped over onto his stomach, not a particularly easy maneuver in a hammock, and huddled beneath the soaked blanket.

This was not working.

He tossed aside the blanket and stumbled to the cockpit, found a tarp and brought it back to the hammock. He unwrapped the tarp and crawled under it.

Better. At least it would keep him dry.

Rain pummeled the tarp, made a mind-numbing tapping noise.

Jeb grunted. Ridiculous. Go belowdecks. Tempted, he turned the idea over. Nice and warm and dry. Safe from potential lightning strikes.

No can do, Stew.

If he went down there, with Haley so close, he knew

he would knock at her door and the way she'd been looking at him over dinner—the way she'd kissed him back when he'd kissed her—told him that if he knocked, she would open that damn door and invite him inside with eager arms.

Haley. Of the strawberry-scented hair and sweet lips. Haley wrapping her arms around his neck, pulling him against her breasts. Haley—

No!

He chuffed out a breath, coughed. His throat felt scratchy. Even through the tarp, he could see the next flash of lightning, felt thunder shake the sailboat. *Seriously, dude, you could get struck by lightning.* No kidding.

Okay, fine. He crawled out of the hammock and went to the cockpit, wadded up into a tarp-covered ball. Not really much of an improvement, but at least the overhang protected him from the main force of the onslaught.

It would pass. It had to pass. Storms always passed.

Rain dripped off the tarp onto his face, rolled down his nose like copious tears. If he went to the lower deck he could just stretch out on the floor. He didn't need a cabin. Haley need never know he was inside.

But *he* would know.

C'mon, you're not that weak. You can be on the same deck as the woman without feeling compelled to seduce her.

That was the thing—whenever he was around her, he couldn't think straight. He wasn't himself. All he wanted to do was touch her.

No, that was a bald-faced lie. He wanted to do a

whole helluva lot more than touch her. Which was what had him so twisted in knots.

Things would change when he saw Jackie again. It had just been too long since he'd seen her. Once he looked in Jackie's eyes, he'd forget all about Haley and he wouldn't regret having kept his hands to himself.

He just had to make it through the night.

More lightning. More thunder. More rain.

Jeb sneezed, shivered. His lungs weighed heavy in his chest. He'd be drier if he took a header into the ocean. He peeked over at the stairs leading to the lower deck. Ten steps away. Twelve, max.

No. He drew the tarp tighter around him. He wasn't going to go down there. The rain would pass.

Eventually. Had to. It hadn't rained for forty days and forty nights since Noah and his ark.

Fifteen minutes later and there was no letup. He couldn't tell if his nose was running or it was just rain, but he felt as lousy as hell. He was *not* going down there. He was determined to prove he could control himself.

In the meantime, his fingers pruned and his head throbbed, but he would gut it out. Not a wimp. Not he. A true sailor could weather the elements, right?

His teeth chattered and he shivered so hard that he couldn't stop. His eyes burned hot, his bones ached and his skin felt waterlogged and tight. He'd never before been accused of being stubborn, but tonight, he stuck to his guns.

An hour later, he couldn't take it anymore. He was too damned exhausted to try anything with Haley anyway. He'd proven his point. Grunting, he heaved himself to his feet, but as he staggered up, his head spun and his knees gave out. The deck rose up to greet him.

Congratulations, Captain, you're officially screwed.

8

Ease—*To let out (a sail or a rope)*

ON WEDNESDAY MORNING, Haley was determined to put the previous day behind her. Fresh start. Yesterday, she'd washed out the dress she'd worn to the party and she put it on again. Even with a T-shirt over the pink bikini, the bathing suit was simply too provocative and she wasn't taking any more chances. Too bad she didn't have a parka and ski pants.

She made two cups of coffee and took them out on the bridge. The sun was up, and in places, water pooled on the deck. Had it rained last night? She thought she'd heard thunder, but she hadn't gotten up to investigate.

Haley reached the top step and from there could see into the cockpit.

Jeb lay facedown on the deck, partially covered by a tarp beaded with water droplets.

Haley gasped, and her fingers loosened. The thick earthenware coffee mugs clattered to the deck. One thumped and rolled, breaking off the handle. The other cracked into two clean pieces. Hot coffee splashed up onto her bare legs, but she scarcely noticed. Her heart vaulted into her throat.

She ran toward him. "Jeb!"

He did not respond.

She yanked the tarp off him, sank onto her knees beside him, her chest tightening, constricting her lungs. Grabbing him by the shoulders, she shook him gently, yet firmly. "Jeb!"

He let out a soft groan.

Dear God, he was burning up!

"Jeb." She patted his cheeks. "Open your eyes."

Slowly, he pried one eye open. "Pretty," he mumbled.

"Pretty what?"

He reached out a finger to touch her lips, but his hand flopped back to his side. "You're pretty," he whispered.

"You've got a fever. Did you sleep outside in the rain?" She narrowed her eyes, put two fingers to the carotid artery at his neck to count his pulse. It was pounding way too fast. "Why did you sleep outside in the rain?"

"Shh." He squeezed his eyes tightly closed. "Headache."

"C'mon." She slipped her hand underneath his armpit. "Let's get you to bed."

A dreamy grin slipped across his face. "Mmm. You, me, bed. Thought you'd never ask."

She managed to lever him into a sitting position. "Not me. Just you. All alone with aspirin and a cool cloth."

He shook his head. "Can't. Gotta sail."

"There will be no sailing today, Captain Whitcomb."

"Gotta get to Key West."

"You said yourself we were ahead of schedule."

"Gotta stop Jackie from marrying that guy."

Her heart pinched. She set her jaw. Seriously, she had to stop being jealous of this Jackie woman. So what if he'd sail with a fever in order to get to her? It was none of Haley's business. "Let's go, Romeo."

"I can sail," he insisted.

"You can't even stand up."

"Can, too."

"Prove it. Do it."

He struggled to his feet. Held out his hands. "Ta-da."

"You're swaying."

"Motion of the ocean, baby."

"Didn't we have a talk about this *baby* thing?"

"Oops." He plastered a palm over his mouth. "Sorry."

She couldn't stop herself from smiling. "Don't apologize. Just don't do it again."

He gave her a little salute and almost toppled over.

"You're drunk with fever."

"You might be right," he admitted.

"Finally," she said, "you're listening to your nurse."

"My nurse." He patted her shoulder.

"I'm not a lapdog."

"Nothing about you is like a lapdog," he agreed. Dark circles smudged his eyes.

She took his elbow and guided him toward the steps, steering him around the spilled coffee and damaged cups.

"Aw, you dropped the coffee."

"Don't worry, I'll clean it up later."

It was slow going. Jeb couldn't seem to pick his legs up. Instead, he shuffled along like a prisoner in shackles.

"Lean on me," she scolded.

"Don't want to."

"Why not? You're not going to overload me. I'm sturdy. I do this kind of thing all the time."

"Because."

"Because why?" Getting him to speak in complete sentences was like pulling teeth. *Don't get irritated. The man's got a fever of at least a hundred and two.*

"I like touching you too much."

Haley sucked in her breath. "Think of me as a nurse, not a woman."

"Kinda hard to do when you're built so nicely," he murmured, but he leaned into her.

She took his weight, wrapped an arm around his muscular waist. The man didn't have an ounce of fat on him, but his shirt was soaked. And his body? Have mercy, it was incredible. "We've got to get you out of these wet clothes."

"Betcha say that to all the guys."

"Stop trying to be charming for two seconds, will you? You're sick."

"Ba—" He cut himself off from saying *baby*. "That's like telling the sun not to shine."

"Hopeless, I know. Here we are at the stairs. Hold on to the rail and we'll take them one step at a time."

"I feel like an idiot."

"You should. Spending the night on the bridge in

a thunderstorm." She clicked her tongue, shook her head. "Don't worry. I won't let you live it down."

"That's what I love about you."

Love? Haley's heart somersaulted. *Chill out, it's a figure of speech.*

"You don't ever let up on anyone."

"That sounds terrible."

"Not terrible at all. You hold people accountable to a higher standard."

Holy Oreos, was she blushing?

"Whoa." Jeb stopped, clung to the rail.

She stopped, too. "Dizzy?"

"Yep."

"Here. Sit." She guided him down to the step.

They sat together, side by side, Jeb breathing fast and shallow. So was she. What the heck was this?

"Deep breath," she instructed herself as much as Jeb.

He took a few deep breaths and so did she. Nodding, he said, "Let's try this again."

It took a full ten minutes, but step by step, they made it to his cabin. Haley directed him to a chair and squatted beside him to slip off his shoes. As a nurse she dressed and undressed patients daily, but this was different. Jeb wasn't her patient and she wasn't his nurse. And even when he was sick, the man turned her on in nine hundred ways.

Today you are his nurse. Be professional.

Easy to say, much harder to do. His skin was thick and healthy. His muscles sublime. Even when he was sick, he was sexy.

She put his shoes aside, stood up. "Arms up."

"What?"

"We've got to get that shirt off you."

"I can do it."

Whew, that was a relief. "Okay." She crossed her arms over her chest, waited for him.

He sat in the chair, managing to look both pale and flushed at the same time. "Give me a minute. I need to rest up."

"Just let me help."

He shook his head. "Okay."

"Can you raise your arms?"

He nodded. "No."

She took the edge of his wet shirt in her hands and slowly rolled it upward. He lifted his arms as she peeled the shirt over taut, tanned abs so delicious they just begged to be licked. She had to bite down on her bottom lip to keep from letting out an appreciative moan.

Finally, she tugged the shirt over his head. His hair stood up in a mussed mess. How endearing he looked. *What? You like your men helpless?*

No, not at all, but illness was the great equalizer. It hit the wealthy and the poor alike.

He slumped against the back of the chair.

She eyed his shorts. Hmm, how to get those off? She could just leave him in them, but they were damp, too. Being wet didn't cause illness—bacteria and viruses did that—but it sure could weaken the immune system, especially since he'd languished outside in the rain all night, while she'd been peacefully curled up in his bed. *Feeling guilty now, huh?*

"Can you take off your pants by yourself?"

"Got it," he said, stood up briefly and then toppled face-first onto the bed.

Right.

"Roll over."

He grunted.

She grabbed his belt loops and tugged him over onto his back. His eyes were closed and he had a slight smile on his face. If he weren't so out of it, she would swear he was enjoying this.

Her fingers went to the snap of his shorts. Instantly, she felt him harden beneath her touch. He didn't move or say a word. His eyes were still closed. What was she going to do now? Undress him or let him sleep in damp shorts?

"Jeb."

He didn't answer.

She poked him with a finger. "Jeb."

He mumbled something barely audible.

Okay, he was out of it. The erection was just a natural response to a woman plucking at his pants. She shouldn't be either pleased or offended by it. Determined to act professionally, she quickly slid his zipper down.

His erection grew.

Beads of sweat popped out on her forehead. She gritted her teeth and pointedly looked away. Moving to the foot of the bed, she grasped the bottom of his shorts with a hand at each leg and tugged them down his hips.

Oops! His underwear came along for the ride and now he was totally naked. Haley hadn't meant to stare. She had no intention of staring. She'd seen any number of naked men in her career as a nurse but she'd never seen anyone like him. Jeb's ego wasn't the only thing that was oversize about the man. Underwear model, hell—he could be a porn star.

Haley curled her fingernails into her palms until it stung. *Put his underwear back on him.*

She hesitated, considered that, then dismissed the idea. Leaving him naked was easier than trying to wrestle him into boxer briefs. The very image brought out goose bumps on her skin. Especially when his erection was jutting up there, proud and tall.

But he was also shivering, his teeth chattering so loudly she could have danced the flamenco to them. His temperature must be on the rise. She covered him with a blanket. He looked miserable, poor guy.

She picked up his wet clothes and hung them up to dry on the towel rack in the bathroom, located aspirin in the medicine cabinets. She roused him enough to make him down two aspirin and forced him to drink a full glass of water before she allowed him to sink back into the covers.

Afterward, she fled to the bridge to clean up the spilled coffee.

When she finished, she straightened and looked out at the wide expanse of deep blue sea. As far as the eye could, see there was nothing but water and seagulls.

It hit her then. How isolated she was. On the ocean with an incapacitated skipper. What if he were desperately ill? She had no medical equipment with her and knew nothing about boats.

Holy Oreos, she was in serious trouble here.

AN ANGEL HAD TAKEN his clothes off.

No, not an angel.

Haley.

Okay, she was something of an angel. He'd admit that. Angel of mercy. *As in have mercy, she's tearing me up!*

Her fingers were cool on his skin, and her hair! So beautiful, the way it fell over her shoulders. She wore it up in that tight bun too much. Her hair should never be restrained. He wanted to touch those beautiful honey-blond strands but his fingers were too shaky.

She leaned over him, smelling of strawberries. He loved strawberries—strawberry shortcake, strawberry jelly, chocolate-covered strawberries, strawberry cake, strawberry Life Savers.

That was Haley. His strawberry lifesaver.

Yum.

Jeb licked his lips. Or at least he tried. His mouth was dry and his lips stuck together. Lip balm. He needed lip balm.

Hey? What was this? A smooth feminine finger was applying slick balm to his lips. What a soft finger. Ah, that felt much better. All he had to do was think about something and it happened. Neat trick.

Test it.

He grinned. He needed an angel in his bed, curled up right next to him, her sweet little fanny pressed up against his pelvis. He needed to run his hands over her curvy hips, trace over the dip of her waist, find the sweet swell of her breasts.

She ran a hand along his spine and he shuddered. Cold. He was so very cold. And hot. Hot and cold all at the same time. Blankets were mounded up on him and he was still so cold, but at the same time he wanted to kick all those covers off and feel the air cool his heated skin.

The covers lifted. There it was. Fresh air.

And the angel!

Sliding underneath the covers with him, curling against him. The push of her firm breasts tight against his shoulder blades.

Was this real? Was she in bed with him?

Or was it, as part of him suspected, nothing more than a very vivid sex dream?

Whatever it was, bring it on. Fantasy, reality, either one, he craved both, more.

She pressed her lips to the nape of his neck.

Jeb growled low in his throat. He was within inches of pounding his chest with his fists and letting out a Tarzan yell of triumph to find himself in bed with her. He turned toward her, dragged her into his arms, kissed her, hard and hot and frantic.

She laughed.

Red-hot electricity straight to his cock.

Heedlessly, he yanked the thin spaghetti straps off her dress, ripped the garment from her body.

The angel gasped, a soft, delighted sound. "Ooh, a caveman. I like that."

"Just wait," he panted.

She wriggled in his arms, the lace of her strapless bra scratching across his chest. The strip of her matching thong panties stretching against her pale skin. He clawed at the fastener on her bra, managed to get it off.

The pulse in his throat throbbed and his cock jumped.

In a feverish daze, Jeb took a deep, steadying breath and placed his hand over her heart. He wanted her. Damn, how he wanted her.

He shouldn't be doing this.

No? Why not?

Because, because…

His head was a mess and he couldn't think of a single reason why he should not be doing this. Need consumed him. He had to have her.

Now!

The way she was kissing him, the angel wanted him right back with a fire and passion that surprised him. She'd had him fooled. He'd thought she was pretty darn regimented, but woo-hoo, he was wrong about that.

She threw her head back, exposed her smooth, creamy neck to him, her honeyed hair trailing down his forearm. She was just as he'd dreamed she'd be— her body was both firm and soft and totally womanly. Her bare breasts rested against his biceps as he gently cupped her in the crook of his arm.

Unless he was dreaming now. It did feel pretty damn surreal.

But how could he be dreaming? She felt so genuine. Smelled so good. Sounded so earthy.

He pulled back, drank her in. Man, he loved the way she looked at him, with wide, knowing eyes.

She lowered her eyelids halfway and gave him a naughty expression. One come-hither glance and he was a goner.

If only he could capture this special moment, lock it in a vault, seal it in a time capsule. He smiled, then laughed and then squeezed her tight. His flesh, from his head to his toes, quivered.

She propped herself up on her elbow and ran a hand through her hair, tousling the long, loose curls. One strand fell saucily across her eye, adding to her sexual mystique. A hazy veil of white light seemed to encompass her.

Was something wrong with his eyes? Or was her halo simply that bright?

Mesmerized, he blinked.

She tucked the wayward tendril behind one ear and batted her lush eyelashes at him. Her blue-eyed gaze snagged his, bright as the Mediterranean. "I'm here to ease your fever."

"If I'm the one with the fever, how come you're so hot?"

Her gaze misted with lust. She flicked out her tongue to lick her full pink lips and Jeb forgot about everything except his driving need to sink deeply into her amazing body.

"Are you just going to stare at me all night?"

"No, ma'am." He crawled on his hands and knees toward her.

She reached up with the flat of her bare foot and pressed it against his chest, halting his progress. The sight of her sweet pink toes shot his desire into overload.

"I'm going to wear you out, Skipper. The way no woman has ever worn you out. Are you prepared for total surrender?" Her sultry laugh skipped across his eardrums.

"Are *you* prepared for everything I'm going to give you?" He narrowed his eyes.

She curled her toes into his chest. "This is a one-shot deal. Let's make it a night to remember."

"Ha! One taste of me and you won't be able to walk away after only one night," he teased, his gaze hooking onto hers.

"Where'd I put my shoes?" she teased right back.

She dropped her foot, curled up to a sitting position and reached for his shoulders.

Jeb groaned.

"Hmm." She reached down to wrap her fingers around his burgeoning shaft. "What have we here?"

His face was level with her breasts. They were gorgeous. Perfect. Full and round and real, but not too big. Just right. The size of navel oranges. He loved navel oranges. He couldn't help reaching out to cup her breasts in his hands.

He lowered his mouth, took one of her pert, straining nipples between his teeth, licked it with his tongue.

Her breath came out in a hot rush, and suddenly, she was as wild and slippery as a dolphin, pulling him down on top of her. Her greedy mouth kissing his cheeks, his chin, the tip of his nose.

Jeb's hunger equaled hers. He melded his mouth against hers and they dissolved into a tumble of arms and legs.

Gotta have her. Gotta have her now.

There was no fighting it.

His dick throbbed. Blood galloped through his veins, engorging him, hard and hot. His mind whirled. He wasn't thinking clearly. Couldn't even think. Primal urge overtook everything else.

Jeb had full command of her lips, but she was ready and waiting for him. She darted her sly, sweet tongue into his mouth, rushing pell-mell past his teeth. This moment rivaled the best day sailing. In fact, the dip and swoop of his blood as it rolled slickly through his veins reminded him of ocean swells.

She ran her fingers up and down his bare back, each

stroke driving the heated urgency inside him higher and higher. How could a guy's temperature be this hot and his brains not fry, his blood not boil?

Aah, wait. He *was* bursting into flames. Rocket ship to Mars. Buckle up and hang on tight.

She raked her fingers through his hair and arched her hips upward, driving him mad with the brush of her nipples beaded tight against his chest and the sight of her sweet honey hair down there—he had to have a taste!

Here I come, baby. No, wait, she didn't like to be called *baby* and he didn't want to call her that. He needed a nickname for her. A term of endearment he'd never used on another woman, but one that fit her perfectly.

Angel.

Good girl, always doing the right thing.

Angel of mercy.

He had to taste her goodness, inhale her and touch every inch of her sweet body. Let her halo light him up inside.

Her lips parted, supple and impatient, mimicking his every move. She dug her fingertips into his spine, squashing his chest against her breasts.

They were nose to nose, Jeb anchoring her to the mattress. He slipped one hand down her inner thigh, searching for her deep heat, finding out how ready she was for him. Gently, he rubbed an index finger along her soft flesh. "Angel."

"Oh, you devil." She sighed.

"You better believe it," he whispered as he found his target and slipped a finger into her.

She trembled beneath his hand.

He shuddered and inched in another finger. When he found her sensitive button with the tip of his thumb, she moaned and pushed her hips up.

She was the most responsive woman he'd ever been with.

"That's right, stud. You're making the earth move for me." She nibbled his earlobe. "But I don't want to do this alone. I want you to come along with me."

"I want this to last."

"All good things must come to an end," she said sagely. "Let's do it up big."

She was too damn wise for his good.

"Come," she whispered and did this crazy thing with her hand, touched some erogenous spot he hadn't known he possessed, and boom! He was off.

He couldn't hold out any longer. He pushed into her. The minute her hot, intimate folds welcomed him, he whispered, "Angel."

Her fingers were in his hair and she was rocking against him, chanting "Jeb" like a mantra.

She stopped breathing then.

Was she about to climax?

No, no, it was too fast. Jeb slowed down, pulled back. "Not yet, angel."

"Don't be contrary." She pouted.

He kissed her forehead, her eyelids, her nose, her cheeks and her chin as she wriggled impatiently beneath him. "You want me to make you come?"

"I want it now!"

"Whatever you say, angel." He dropped his feet to the floor, pulled her to the edge of the mattress. The tip of his throbbing erection hovered just outside her sweet sex. She spread her thighs apart and he nudged against her entrance.

He looked down at her naked body through the golden haze of enchantment. Her lips were pink and shiny, her hair mussed, her breasts full and luscious. Damn, but she was the sexiest woman he'd ever known.

Haley writhed against him. "Get inside me now, Skipper, before this boat runs aground."

"I can't deny you anything." He sank into her.

Haley held his hips and drew him in deeper.

They let out twin sighs.

The heat, the rocking of the boat, the heady smell of their combined sex pushed them over the edge. A few powerful thrusts and they were both lost at sea. Jeb came inside her at the same moment that Haley cried out in pleasure.

Exhausted, he clung to her, carried her with him as he rolled over onto his back. She lay on top of him now, peered down into his eyes.

Magic.

He'd always loved sex, but it had never felt like this. Freaking abracadabra magic.

Her hair trailed across his face, the scent of strawberries. He inhaled deeply, closed his eyes. Best thing. She was the best thing that had ever happened to him.

The heat ebbed away, but the glow in his heart flared brilliant and bright.

He reached to kiss her, but she was gone, and his hand hit cool, empty sheet. *Playing hide-and-seek, you little minx. Here I come.*

The pun made him smile. He opened his eyes.

Haley stood in the door, fully clothed, a tray in

her hand and a concerned frown furrowing her pretty forehead.

Don't frown, angel.

"Are you all right? You were making the most dreadful moaning sounds." She set the tray on the desktop, stepped over to the bed.

"What are you doing dressed?" he asked and tried to give her a rakish grin, but feared he came off looking like a sloppy drunk. His smile slipped.

She shrugged. "As if I'd be naked with you."

"You were, just two minutes ago. How'd you get dressed so fast?"

"What are you talking about?" She stepped forward, but stopped abruptly. "Wait a minute!"

Ah, crap!

She pressed her lips together and her eyes twinkled. "Were you having a sex dream?"

"No, no," he denied.

"Yes, yes." She snapped her fingers, clearly enjoying his embarrassment. "That's what all the moaning was about. If I'd known I wouldn't have interrupted you."

His chest tightened. All of that beautiful lovemaking nothing more than a fabulous dream. He forced a devil-may-care laugh. He wasn't embarrassed. By sex? No, siree. Not he. Sex was normal. Natural. *You thought you were really having sex with her.* It had felt so damned real. How could a dream feel so real?

"You *were* having a sex dream. About me. About us."

His face flamed. Jeb lowered his head. Dummy. He thought a sex dream was real. How could he have been so fooled?

"It's okay." She chuckled softly. "While I'm deeply flattered to be part of your sexual fantasies, it was all fever-induced. Nothing to be ashamed of. It happens. Simple biology."

"Just a fever." His body felt heavy and his heart shrunk in his chest. "Nothing but a fever."

She leaned over to press a palm against his forehead. It was all he could do not to twist away from her touch. "Your fever's gone. Don't worry, I'm sure the naughty dreams are gone with it."

Yes. Jeb gulped. That was exactly what he feared.

9

Telltales—*Yarn or ribbons on the luff of a sail to help with trimming*

"I MADE CHICKEN NOODLE SOUP from scratch," she said efficiently, professionally. Nurse mode. That was the best way to deal with this. It wasn't the first time she'd witnessed a patient having a fever-fueled sex dream, but as far as she knew, it was the first time she'd had a starring role in one.

"You made me soup?" Jeb's eyes widened in disbelief and he shook his head slowly. "That takes hours."

"Don't look so amazed. It's not like I had much else to do." She leaned over and fixed the blanket. She curled her bare toes against the sleek wood floor. *Stay grounded.*

She tried not to notice his bare chest—ha, as if she could—and tucked the covers underneath Jeb's arms. The man could be a swimsuit model, no doubt about it.

He wriggled.

Hey, buddy, I'm just as uncomfortable about this as you are.

Straightening, she smiled. Put on a happy face. It worked for him—why not give it a shot?

"You're spoiling me."

"You should be very accustomed to that." She picked up the legged tray, carried it to the bed and positioned it over his lap. She unfolded a paper napkin and spread it over his bare chest. There. Covered that dangerous puppy up.

"Mostly from people that I pay to spoil me. Not too many people do it for me spontaneously from the goodness of their generous heart."

"What about your mother? Surely she spoiled you."

"She paid the servants to spoil me. Does that count?" he quipped.

"Get out the violins for the poor little rich boy."

A fleeting look of sadness flickered in his eyes, but he quickly snuffed it out with a wide smile. He might have had a plush childhood, but she had a sense that he'd gotten lost in the shuffle of multiple marriages and divorces and blended families. Was that why it was so easy for him to go with the flow? She admired that trait. How he didn't let bumps in the road keep him from enjoying life. If only she could be more like him in that way.

"Usually, I'm the one doing the spoiling," he said.

"You are the one with the money," she pointed out.

"Why do I get the feeling that's a bad thing in your eyes?"

She shrugged, sat down on the edge of the bed. Which was odd because nurses were trained not to sit on their patients' beds. It went against everything she'd been taught, but here she was sitting on his bed. He was not her patient, after all. Rationalization did not excuse the behavior. She didn't understand why she didn't get up. "Money's not bad. It's the frivolous waste of it that gets to me."

"Like ordering important equipment instead of splurging on a pretty solarium," he said.

He was bringing that up, huh? "Well, now that you've mentioned it, yes. Solariums are nice, but not necessary. Medical equipment is a must-have."

"The patients enjoy the solarium. Boosts their spirits and a happy patient is a healthy patient."

"They live on an island. All you have to do is raise a window. No need for specific architecture that costs extra money."

"You got your equipment."

"Only after I butted heads with you. Everyone else was so eager to kiss your backside."

"Because I was the guy with the wallet."

"Don't you get tired of it?"

"What?"

"Having people like you only because you have money."

He pretended to pout. "Is that the reason? I thought it was my charm and devastating good looks."

"Are you fishing for compliments?"

"That meeting was the first time I realized just how special you were."

She ducked her head, slanted him a sideways glance. "Because I ticked you off?"

"You were the one who was ticked off," he reminded her. "I was amused. You become passionate so easily." He tracked a knowing gaze over her. "You've got a fire inside you, Haley French."

She crossed her arms over her chest so he couldn't

see the way her body was reacting under his scrutiny. "Eat your soup before it gets cold."

"Are you ever off duty, nurse?"

"It's ingrained in me. What can I say? Are you going to make me feed you?"

He raised his eyebrows. "I like the sound of that."

She snorted. "You would."

"What do you have against men with money?"

"It's not the money, per se. It's the way money makes them feel entitled. As if they can have whatever they want."

"What was his name?" Jeb asked.

"Who?"

"The rich guy who broke your heart."

Haley's eyes widened. How had he guessed? Bile burned a toxic path up her throat at the memory of Trey Goss. For the most part, she'd managed to put the past behind her. She didn't like dwelling on something she could not change. "Who says a rich guy broke my heart?"

"Why else would you have such a chip on your shoulder for wealthy men?"

"Eat."

He saluted her, picked up the soupspoon and pushed around chunks of chicken, carrots, celery, onions and egg noodles in the steamy broth. He took a few bites. "Mmm, this is really good."

Why was she still sitting here? She had no answer. No excuse other than she wanted to make sure he ate. He needed nourishment. That was the only reason. "I'm glad you like it."

"You're not eating anything?"

"I had some soup before I brought it in to you."

He ate every last drop with gusto. Great. That was a good sign. He was on the road to recovery. It was probably just one of those twenty-four-hour things. If he kept improving, she'd let him sail tomorrow.

"What time is it?" he asked.

"Four in the afternoon."

He looked relieved. "That's not so bad. We were a day ahead of schedule, so even losing a day, we should still hit Key West by early Saturday morning as long as the weather cooperates."

"It's four in the afternoon on *Wednesday*," she said. "You've been asleep since yesterday morning."

"What!" He shoved the tray at her. "Here, take this."

She stood, picked up the tray.

"We'll have to sail through the night."

"You're not sailing anywhere tonight."

"Who's gonna stop me?"

"I am."

"And how do you plan on doing that?"

"By holding your clothes hostage."

"Then I'll just sail naked." Jeb swung his legs over the edge of the bed and, thankfully, kept the covers over his lap, but she couldn't avoid that bare chest.

Oh, gosh, if he stood up, she would see his full naked body again. Unprepared. She was woefully unprepared for this, for him. "You're too weak—"

He inhaled audibly, grabbed his head and muttered, "Whoa."

She settled the tray onto the desk and then turned to press him back against the pillow, making sure to keep the covers over him. "Lie down."

"I'm okay. Just sat up a bit too fast."

"You're getting better, but you're in no condition to sail and your body is trying to tell you that."

"Ever thought about becoming a drill sergeant? You'd be really good at it."

"I'm looking after your best interests."

"You know," he said, "if someone else uttered that line, I wouldn't believe them, but you…"

"But me what?"

"You really do put other people's interests ahead of your own. You really do care."

"You sound surprised."

"I'm surprised because there aren't many people like you in the world."

She rearranged his covers again. Her heart did a crazy dip-swirl thing. He seemed to know exactly what to say to flatter her. He truly had a gift for soft soap. *Lather me up.* "There are more than you think."

"You're too generous."

"And you," she said sternly, "need to learn to ride out the consequences of your choices."

"What does that mean?"

"You chose to spend the night in the rain and you got sick. You can't get well on demand."

"You're blaming me for getting sick?"

"No, I'm saying you have to accept the consequences of your actions."

"That's harsh."

"That's reality. You have a tendency toward magical thinking, Jeb."

He looked as if she'd just run him through with a skewer. "Wow."

"I'm not saying this to hurt your feelings."

"You didn't hurt my feelings. It's just that…" He trailed off.

"What?"

"You see right through me. Am I that transparent?"

"To anyone who's really looking at you."

"You see me as I am, huh?"

"I believe I do."

"And you still like me?"

"Who wouldn't like you?"

"My point exactly." He paused a long moment. "I've always believed I could do anything I set my mind to. You'd probably say it's because I grew up privileged, and maybe you'd be right, but I seemed to have the ability to get what I wanted with a smile."

The man did have a devastating smile.

"It never seems to work with you, though."

"I wouldn't say never."

He smiled then, big and playful.

And she fell for it. Smiled back. Hey, smiling wasn't going to hurt anything.

"You've got a point."

"You agree with me?"

"When I was six or seven, I got it into my head that I could live in the water like a dolphin. My dad had a waterfront home, Tampa Bay—this was between wife number two and wife number three—and I'd spend summers with him. My dad has this pedal boat for us kids to play on, and one day after I'd gotten in trouble for something, I decided I was going to go live with my real family, the dolphins. So I pedaled out into the bay."

"Alone?" Her insides tightened. She could just see him as a kid, totally heedless to the danger he was putting himself in. He must have driven his mother crazy with worry.

"Well, yeah. If I was going to go live with the dolphins, I didn't want to take any people along with me. That would defeat the point. I was just about to dive off the boat when I thought it might be a good idea to anchor the pedal boat, just in case I couldn't find the dolphins right off the bat."

"This story is making me nervous." She nibbled her bottom lip.

"Clearly," he said, "I survived, so settle down, worrywart. I pedaled back to the house, got a cinder block, tied a rope around it, stuck it on the pedal boat and went back out."

"And you were just six or seven?" She wrung her hands. "Where were your parents?"

He shrugged. "They were pretty lax."

She shook her head. No child of hers would ever be given such a free rein at such a young age.

"I dropped anchor. I was convinced that I was going to find a school of dolphins and swim away with them. I totally believed it deep down in my bones."

What an imaginative and adventuresome kid he'd been. Haley was hooked on the horns of his narrative. He had a way of spinning a story that reeled her in. He'd make a great salesman.

"I held my breath and dived in headfirst. Everything around me was dark and cold."

But of course. Jeb would never just dip his toe into something and ease into it.

"And I was really shocked when I couldn't stay under. I tried, but the water pushed against me and I just had to breathe. I tried to breathe underwater, but of course, I got a mouthful of ocean. Then it occurred to me that the reason I couldn't do it, couldn't breathe, couldn't find my dolphin family was because I'd anchored that pedal boat and if I hadn't had a fallback plan, then I would have been able to swim away underwater. I'd ruined my chances by casting a safety net, by not trusting in the magic."

"Did you try it without anchoring the boat?"

He shook his head. "My dad found me and I got a good bawling out. Not long after that, he sold the beach house, but honestly, I believed it was because my lack of belief had blown my chances forever."

"And yet you named your boat *Second Chance*."

A smile played at his lips. "I did, at that."

"You need to get some rest." She picked up the tray, moved to the door with it.

"You're not going to leave me here alone, are you?"

"That's the idea."

"I'm bored."

Honestly, so was she. She'd spent the past day reading ebooks on her cell phone in between checking in on him. She was more than ready for conversation.

"I've got some board games underneath the bench seating of the dining room table," he said. "Pick your favorite."

She was tempted. "If you promise to be good."

"Define *good*." He grinned impishly.

"Not getting up until I say you can."

"Not sure I can keep that promise." The sexy look on his face told her he was thinking of an alternate meaning for the word *up*.

Her cheeks burned. She sat down the tray, opened a drawer, pulled out underwear, cargo shorts and a T-shirt for him and tossed them at him. "Put these on and I'll think about playing a game with you."

"Don't think too hard, angel. That's your problem—you think too much."

"And your problem is that you don't think enough."

"Makes us a perfect match," he teased. "Two halves of a whole."

She picked up the tray again. "I wonder what your friend Jackie would have to say about that." Then she turned and walked out the door, blood pumping hot and fast through her veins.

JEB GOT DRESSED in the clothes that Haley had thrown at him and he waited for her return.

And waited.

And waited.

And waited.

An hour later, when he assumed she was just going to leave him hanging, a sharp knock sounded on the door, but she didn't wait for him to invite her in. Instead, she entered, carrying an armful of board games.

"I've never heard of any of these games before. Don't you have Monopoly or Scrabble or Parcheesi?"

"Nope."

She set the board games on the bed. "You pick one."

"Ah," he said, slipping the bottom game from the stack. "This one."

"'I've Never,'" she said, reading the name of the game, "'The Outrageous Game of Truth.' Hmm. Sounds interesting. I'm in."

"Actually, it's a drinking game. You need hooch."

"Well, I'm not going to let you drink. You're just recovering from a fever."

"Think of it as medicinal, Scotch and water, with lots of water so I don't dehydrate? Besides, I never lose at this game. You'll be the one doing all the drinking."

"Oh, ho, that sounds like a challenge to me. Consider the gauntlet thrown," she said. "I'm very competitive."

"So I've noticed. The liquor is underneath the bar."

She left and came back a few minutes later with a bottle of peach brandy and two tumblers. She poured an inch into each glass. "Sip when you lose."

"I'm not going to lose."

"We'll see," she said, giving him a knowing look that was so adorable he almost laughed. "How do you play this thing?"

"It's pretty simple. You roll the dice, move to that numbered square on the board and if the question written on the square is true, then you move forward a space. If it's not true, you have to take a drink, then roll the dice again for your next move."

"What's to keep someone from lying?"

"I don't lie. Do you?"

"No. This is a hypothetical question."

"If you're caught in a lie and you're called on it, you have to drink twice."

"Hmm, so this game turns you into a drunken liar."

"Only if you don't tell the truth."

"I'm ready to whip your butt," she said, rolling the dice between her palms as he opened the board up on the bed between them. She rolled a three, moved her game piece forward three spaces and leaned over to read what was written there.

"Hey," she said. "These questions are all of an adult nature."

"That's the game." He gave her a knowing wink. "Too much for you? We could always play Old Maid."

"Are you saying I'm a prude?"

"You *are* blushing."

"Fine." She ran a hand through her hair and pressed her lips into a prim line and then read the question on the game board. "'I've never been spanked in foreplay.'"

Jeb chuckled. He'd bet a thousand dollars that Haley had never done anything that outside-the-box. Not that a little spanking was very kinky. "True or false, angel? If it's true, you get to move forward one square. If it's false, you have to take a drink."

Hesitantly, she took a sip of brandy.

"Look at you," Jeb hooted. "Haley likes having her butt spanked. No wonder you wanted to whip mine."

"I didn't say I liked it." She tossed her head, but her cheeks reddened considerably. "Go on. It's your turn."

Jeb rolled. Landed on six. "'I've never had a threesome,'" he read.

"True or false?"

He moved ahead one square.

Haley snapped her fingers. "I challenge that. I say you're lying."

His eyes met hers. "I might have been something of a player before this past year, but I've never been to bed with more than one woman at a time." He purposefully held her gaze longer than he should have. Was it bad of him to tease her? "When I'm with a woman, she gets my full, undivided attention."

Haley gulped visibly, dropped his gaze as if it was plutonium.

"Take a drink," he said.

"Why?"

"If you challenge someone and they're not lying, then *you* have to take a drink."

"You didn't explain that in the beginning."

"I'm explaining it now."

She rolled the dice with a shaky hand. "'I've never been arrested.'" With a disgruntled look, she took another sip of brandy. "At this rate I'll be blitzed before we're halfway through the game."

Wow, he would never have expected this. "Quite the little jailbird, are we?"

She held back her shoulders in a cocky gesture. "What? It was a protest rally."

He read the square he'd landed on. "'I've never had sex on a water bed.' Nope, never done that, either."

"But you've had sex on a bed on the water," she pointed out.

"That's not what the question asked."

"I challenge that one, too."

"Haley, Haley, Haley. How old do you think I am? I wasn't born in the seventies at the height of the water bed craze."

"Well, neither was I, and I've slept on a water bed."

"But did you have sex on it?"

"No, but it's not my question."

"Touché. Take a drink."

"Why?"

"I wasn't lying and you challenged me."

She chuffed out a breath and took a sip so small she barely got her lips wet. "Fine. Happy now?"

He nodded. "Very."

"My turn." She tossed the dice again. Moved up two spaces. She was ahead of him on the board and on drinking. "'I've never drunk-texted an ex.' Ha! At last something I haven't done."

Jeb took his turn. "'I've never streaked.' Okay, I have done that." He took a swallow of brandy.

"You streaked?"

"Uh-huh."

"Where?"

"College graduation."

"Seriously?" She squealed.

"Not one of my finest moments, but yeah. It was a dare."

"And if the person had dared you to jump off a building, would you have done it?"

"Now you sound like my mother."

"I can't believe you streaked. How embarrassing."

"Hey, I didn't get caught. No arrests on my record, Miss Jailbird."

Haley read her next question. "'I've never slept with a married person.'"

A strange look came over her face and she peeked over at him.

It hit Jeb like a punch to the gut and he just knew she was going to lie.

"Nope, never did that." She moved her marker up one space.

He should let it go. No matter that his gut was telling him that she was lying, it was none of his business. It was a stupid game.

"Challenge," he said in a voice so steely it surprised him.

She startled. "Pardon?"

"I challenge. I think you *have* slept with a married man." Why did he care? Why was he suddenly so pissed off?

Her color instantly paled. "I don't want to play this game anymore." She hopped off the bed.

Jeb wasn't going to let her get away with that. He grabbed her by the elbow. "Haley?"

She yanked against his grip, but he didn't let go.

"Talk to me."

Tears brimmed in her eyes and it just about undid him. Immediately, he let go of her. What had happened?

She ducked her head, turned away and gave him her back.

"Never mind. I shouldn't have pressed. It's none of my business." He swept the game board and pieces back into the box. Why had he ruined a perfectly nice evening?

"I lied because I'm so ashamed of myself," she mumbled. "I didn't know he was married when we began the affair."

"Was it the rich guy? The one that prejudiced you against people with money?"

Mutely, she nodded.

Jeb had an impulse to hunt the guy down and punch his lights out for hurting Haley.

"That's why it gets all over me when you call me *baby*. He called me *baby*. Like I was a child, an infant. Of course, I really was as naive as a baby. I took people at face value. I thought if someone treated you nicely that it meant they were a nice person."

"Looks can be deceiving." Seriously, he was dishing up trite adages for her? Jeb clenched his teeth. He didn't know what else to say.

"It's the one thing in my life I regret most. I let myself down." She cried quietly, her shoulders trembling.

"Shh," he murmured and reached for her.

With her back still to him, she wilted onto the mattress. "Don't be so nice to me. I don't deserve it."

"You broke up with him when you found out he was married, right?"

She stiffened and a sick feeling settled in the pit of his stomach. She hadn't left the relationship when she'd learned he was married. Wow. So his idol had feet of clay after all. It was like finding out that the America's Cup trophy was made out of aluminum instead of sterling silver. How long had he had her up on a pedestal?

"I tried to break up with him," she whispered, "but that night…" She put a hand to her mouth, shook her head.

"Haley." He rubbed her back. "You don't have to tell me anything. You owe me no explanations."

She dropped her forehead to his shoulder and sobbed helplessly.

He wrapped his arm around her waist, drew her against him. Oh, damn…oh, hell. *Don't cry, angel, don't cry.* What had he started? "You loved him a lot, huh?"

She shook her head. "No, no, that's not it at all."

He hooked his thumb underneath her chin and gently guided it up until she was forced to meet his gaze. It killed him to see her looking so wrecked.

"It's okay. Whatever happened, it's okay now. You're here with me and you're safe." He pressed his lips against her forehead, but that only made her cry harder.

"He…" She swallowed. "He said we weren't done until *he* said we were done. That's when he…forced me into bed. I said no, but he was bigger and stronger, and in the end, I just stopped fighting. I wanted the whole thing over with."

"Are you saying he raped you?"

Silently, she nodded.

"You didn't report it to the police?"

"I did, but the D.A. said there wasn't evidence to bring the case to trial. Ultimately, it would have been my word against the word of a wealthy, prominent businessman, and I had been having an adulterous affair with him. I could tell the authorities didn't really believe my story." She buried her face in her hands.

Adrenaline shot through Jeb. His impulse to punch the guy turned dark and deadly. He wanted to strangle the son of a bitch with his bare hands. Flat-out kill him for hurting Haley. He had no idea he could feel so murderous. He was an easygoing guy. He didn't get enraged. But this…this was unforgivable behavior. Stringing the man up was too good for him.

Haley's tears dampened his shirt. He ran his hand through her hair, held her close, kissed her forehead again and again, softly and sweetly. Nothing sexual. Total comfort. The last thing she needed was some horny guy pawing at her. He reached for a tissue on the shelf above the headboard and handed it to her.

She dabbed her eyes. "I don't know why I'm crying about this. It was years ago. I was a freshman in college. Young and dumb, as they say."

"No, not dumb. Don't put this on yourself."

"Honestly, I sort of felt like I deserved the punishment. I should have suspected he was married."

"Haley!" How could she think that?

"I felt guilty and ashamed for having such poor judgment."

"You did *not* deserve that!"

"If I'd been smarter—"

"Shh, shh." He cradled her in his arms.

"I went to counseling," she said. "I thought I'd put it all behind me, but apparently there's still some lingering issues."

"Ah, damn, angel, I'm so sorry."

"It's not your fault. You didn't do anything, but in a way you remind me of him. In the beginning anyway, before I got to really know you."

Jeb gritted his teeth. "I hate that I remind you of him. No wonder you disliked me."

"It's not you." She shook her head. "It's me. I'm gun-shy—"

"Understandably."

"And I was terrified of getting involved with that kind of man again."

"I'm not like that. I would never, ever hurt you, Haley." He tipped her chin up, and she met his eyes.

"I know, I know, but there's Jackie. I know you're not married to her, but you want to be."

Yeah. Jackie. Jeb blew out his breath. He wasn't going to think about that for now. For now, he just wanted to comfort Haley. He rubbed a palm against her upper back. "If you want to keep talking, I'm all ears, but if you'd rather not say any more, I understand."

Haley let out a small sigh. "Honestly, I'm glad I told you. I feel better already. You're a great listener, Jeb."

"Anything else I can do?"

"Listening is enough. Thank you for that."

"I wish I could do more."

"The past is the past, and I've put it behind me," she said, sounding determined. "Let's focus on something else."

"What would you like to talk about?" he asked.

"Sailing," she replied staunchly. "The sailing bug has bitten me and I'm fascinated."

Now, that was a topic he could handle. "Anything specific you'd like to discuss?"

"Could you show me how to use navigation charts to plot a sea voyage?"

"Love to. We need to do a dead reckoning anyway."

"Dead reckoning? What's that?"

"It's how we figure out where we are and where we're going from here."

"Sounds very purposeful." She smiled. The dark emotions that had earlier clouded her eyes had vanished completely. "Let's do it."

That plucky, hopeful smile tugged his heartstrings. He admired her so much. Admired the way she was able to deal with such adversity and not let it cripple her. She was amazing.

You're in trouble now, Whitcomb. She's gotcha wrapped around her sweet little finger like a telltale.

10

Dead reckoning—*Plotting your course based on the distance from a previously known position*

ON THURSDAY MORNING, they set sail at dawn. With Jeb's dead reckoning and the happy discovery that the wind was still at their backs, he predicted that if everything went smoothly, even with factoring in the delay, they could still make Key West by Saturday morning. It still gave them plenty of time to get through customs before Jackie's 4:00 p.m. wedding.

For her part, Haley tried not to think about how good it had felt to tell Jeb her secret. He'd been so kind, so understanding, so comforting, and he'd made her feel— Well, she wasn't going to analyze that.

The day had passed companionably. Jeb recovered so quickly it was almost as if he'd never been stricken with a fever, and Haley took him up on his offer to teach her more sailing tips, tricks and techniques. He guided her in taking the helm and she learned how to make the boat go faster through steering. Jeb's lesson there was "steer straight to steer fast." She learned about weather helm, which was a sailboat's tendency to turn toward the wind, and about all the forces pushing and pulling on it.

What surprised her most was that the boat pilot had to make small steering changes in order to keep a sailboat going straight. Whenever the wind changed in velocity or the boat shifted its angle of heel—she'd learned that *heel* was the term used for when a sailboat leaned or tipped to one side—the amount of weather helm changed, forcing the pilot to alter the rudder slightly to stay the course, but by the end of the day, she was already getting the feel of it.

They kept their conversations neutral, steering off hot-button topics like sex. Instead, they discussed books that they loved and they were delighted to discover they had the same taste in literature; both of them enjoyed hard-boiled detective stories, spine-tingling thrillers and biographies. They talked about St. Michael's and what they loved most about the island. They veered into other topics—childhood pets, vacations they'd taken, how to make perfect homemade ice cream.

The day passed pleasantly punctuated by salty sea air and a bracing wind that sent them soaring toward Florida. They stayed up late, lingering over the pasta dinner Jeb cooked and a nice bottle of Chianti, then they went to their separate sleeping quarters, neither one of them brave enough to act on the sexual feelings sparking between them.

By Friday morning, Haley found her entire perception of Jeb had shifted. Whereas before she'd really gotten to know him she'd thought he was frivolous and a bit full of himself, now she'd learned that he simply didn't like to dwell on the darker side of life and he had a talent for turning work into play. Who could fault him for that? It was a skill she sorely needed to learn.

He had a gifted way of making ordinary tasks enjoyable. No wonder everyone wanted to hang around him. And he made her feel entertained, dazzled and inspired. His unwavering self-confidence had a way of filling up the gaps inside her.

"I'm jealous of your self-discipline," he told her as they hoisted the sail at dawn.

"I'm envious of your ability to turn everything into a game." She pushed a strand of windblown hair back off her face. She hadn't once pulled her hair into a ponytail or bun since she'd come on board his boat. Having her hair down made her feel freer, easygoing. "And I thought you found me stick-in-the-muddish."

"I'm serious," he said. "You make me feel inadequate in that regard."

"Jeb, I don't mean to make you feel that way."

"You also make me feel like I have a higher calling and I don't want to let you down."

She thumped him lightly on the chest. "Just live up to your full potential."

"Is that all I have to do to win your respect?"

"You already have my respect."

His eyes twinkled with amusement. "When did I earn that?"

"It started the day you rescued the seagull, but it hit home when you told me how much you wanted to change in order to win Jackie back. I respect people who try to improve."

"You're a fair and honest woman, Haley French."

They stood looking at each other, the wind whipping around them. It was the most perfect moment, the two of them sharing a smile, a sail and their appreciation for each other.

"You know, I've had a really good time this week," she said. "In spite of the unconventional beginning."

"Me, too."

"I'm almost sorry it'll be over tomorrow."

"Almost?" he asked.

"Well, you know me. I can only live in a fantasy for so long. Sooner or later I have to roll up my sleeves and get back to work. Too much time in paradise makes me antsy."

He flashed her a row of his perfect teeth, gave that jaunty wink of his as the wind caught the mainsail and they were off. They'd been sailing for a little less than an hour when land came into view for the first time since they'd left St. Michael's.

"What's that?" Haley pointed.

"Pelican Island. It's a ghost island."

"What's a ghost island?"

"You know, like a ghost town. Once upon a time the island was inhabited, but a hurricane in the early 1900s wiped out everything but the lighthouse."

"I love lighthouses."

"I've always wanted to go ashore. The lighthouse is a popular rendezvous spot for people sailing from the Bahamas to Florida. Too bad we don't have time to stop and investigate."

"Too bad," Haley echoed.

"But we'll be sailing right by it. You'll get a close view of the lighthouse."

She left the sailing to Jeb and went to the bow of the boat as the *Second Chance* glided toward the island. The past few days had been an eye-opener. When she'd first found herself accidentally stowed away upon Jeb's boat, she had not expected to come out of this experience feeling…*cleansed*.

Her time at sea had been restorative, a mental vacation she hadn't even known she'd needed. Being out here on the open sea surrounded by nature reminded her of her own buried wildness. She loved the feel of sunshine on her face and the waves rocking beneath her feet. She was alert to life, fully awake to new experiences in a way she'd never quite been before, and it was all due to Jeb.

She darted a glance over her shoulder at him. He looked so commandingly masculine as his hands skillfully guided the boat. In the deepest, darkest, most intimate, most honest part of her, her muscles clenched in an ache so sweet and sharp, she had to close her eyes, moisten her lips.

He held the keys to a universe of sensations and delight. The man knew how to play. He was a sensualist. A gastronome. No doubt about it. Emotions flooded her. Feelings she'd kept carefully in check since she'd made a youthful mistake and fallen for the wrong man.

Was she doing it again?

Yes. Not because Jeb wasn't a good guy, but rather because his heart belonged to someone else. Haley could not, would not fall for him, but as strong-minded as she was, she could not seem to control her body's internal response. No amount of chiding could stop her smiling every time he looked deeply into her eyes.

Resolutely, she directed her attention back to the sea, and within an hour, they were upon Pelican Island.

The lighthouse jutted on a rock pier. Images of a

lonely lighthouse keeper swept into her mind. She could see him manning the light that kept boats from crashing into the island. Lighthouses were the stuff of romantic legends and lore—mermaids and sirens and hapless sailors dashed to death on rocky shoals.

The island was shaped like a crescent roll, a small inlet sheltering lighter blue water. She spied some kind of creature moving in the bay.

Was it a dolphin?

Haley squinted. No, the creature was too large for that and too slow, as well. It bobbled on the water, bigger than a cow, gray and lumpish. Elephant. It looked like an underwater elephant without the trunk.

A manatee!

It was one of Florida's famous manatees.

The thrill sent a shiver over her and she ran to Jeb.

"What's got you grinning?"

She put out her hand. "Binoculars."

"What is it?"

"I think there's a manatee over by the lighthouse."

"You sure it's not a ghost?" he teased, digging around in the box where he stowed his sailing gear and coming up with a pair of high-powered binoculars in a black waterproof case.

"There's no such thing as ghosts," she scoffed and hurriedly returned to the bow. She opened the case, took out the binoculars, brought them to her eyes and fine-tuned the focus. It took her a minute to find the creature.

Yes! It was a manatee, big and docile.

The manatee swam above water with lumbering movements, propelling itself forward a few feet and then disappearing from sight as it sank below the water. It came up for air a few seconds later in the exact spot that it had been before. It thrashed. Vanished again. The manatee surfaced once more, swam, submerged, repeating the process again and again.

Something was wrong.

She frowned. Tried to enhance the view by fiddling with the lenses, took another look. Was that a thin black wire wrapped around the manatee? Or was she seeing things?

"Jeb!" She waved him over.

He engaged the autohelm feature and came strolling toward her. Her pulse jumped and she swallowed past the lump filling her throat.

"What is it?"

"Look there and see if I'm imagining things." She passed him the binoculars. "I think the manatee has gotten something wrapped around him and he's trapped."

Jeb raised the binoculars to his eyes and studied the creature for a long moment. The wind whipped his cargo shorts around his tanned legs. He looked like summer. Clean and hot and lazy. Haley's mouth watered.

"I believe you might be right."

"What is it? Can you tell?"

"Not from this distance."

"What are we going to do?"

Jeb lowered the binoculars. "We're not going to do anything. Nothing we can do. Manatees are really big."

"But I heard they're very gentle."

"Haley, it's just not feasible. Logistically, it will be a nightmare trying to land the sailboat on those rocky shoals."

"Couldn't we anchor out here and swim to shore?"

"That sounds a lot easier than it is. The current is swift and unless you're a strong swimmer—"

"I am."

"We don't know that we can rescue him. We're not equipped for manatee rescue."

"We have to try. We just can't go off and leave him like this."

"I'll get on the radio and let the Coast Guard know. They'll send someone out."

"That could take hours. The poor thing could die by then. It's already exhausted itself."

"Haley," he said softly, "you can't save the entire world."

She snapped her mouth shut, crossed her arms and narrowed her eyes.

"You're giving me the stink eye?" he said.

"You deserve it."

"For what?"

"Oh, I get it."

He looked puzzled. "Get what?"

"You think it would take up too much time to help the manatee."

"Well, it would, with absolutely no guarantee of success. Plus, we'll be putting our own lives in danger. Much safer for both us and the manatee to let the Coast Guard handle it."

"You mean much easier for you. If we stopped it might keep you from preventing Jackie from getting married."

"Yes, there is that. It is the reason we're out here in the first place."

She couldn't believe he was being so rational. This

was the same impulsive guy who'd rescued the seagull with the plastic beer ring around its feet? "You're deluding yourself, you know," she muttered.

"In what way?"

"Jackie."

"Are you trying to pick a fight?"

Was she? "You think that just because you come sailing up, all Benjamin Braddock from *The Graduate,* begging her to run away from her wedding with you that she's going to do it."

The expression on his face told her she'd nailed it.

"News flash, if she wanted to marry you, she would never have broken up with you."

"She might not have wanted to marry the old me, but when she hears what I've done, she'll change her mind," he said stubbornly.

"That's magical thinking, Jeb. Can't you just accept the fact that she's in love with this other guy?"

His chin hardened and all the smile went out of his eyes. Haley had never seen him looking so bleak. "She just thinks she's in love with him."

Her stomach hurt. She put a palm over her belly. "How do you know that?"

"Because she's supposed to be with me."

"How do you know *that?*"

"Because she promised she'd give me a year and she didn't give me a full year. That's not like Jackie to go back on her word."

"My point exactly. Doesn't it strike you that this guy must be awfully special for her not to even tell you she's getting married, just sends you a text invitation, which, FYI, probably means she didn't really expect you to come?" Okay, so she felt as if she was ruining Christmas, but come on, it had to be said.

"Then why did she tell me at all? She could have just gotten married and let me find out about it after the fact. I think she was secretly wanting me to swoop in and sail her away."

"You've got some very romantic notions about women," Haley said. "Jackie probably told you about the wedding because you're a childhood friend that she cares about. She wants you there to celebrate her joy, not to break it up."

Anger flashed in his eyes. "You don't even know her."

Haley held up her palms. "You're right, but I also know that for all your devil-may-care attitude, you're not the kind of guy to leave a helpless animal behind when you could help it out. You did come to St. Michael's after all and almost single-handedly saved that island. Your motives might not have been the most altruistic, but what you did was admirable."

"Dammit." He snorted and stalked away.

"Where are you going?" she called after him.

"To drop anchor. Go put on that pink bikini, angel. We're going to save a manatee."

HALF AN HOUR LATER, with the *Second Chance* bobbing and anchored forty yards offshore, Jeb and Haley swam for the small bay where the manatee floundered. They'd swam rather than take the *Second Chance*'s inflatable dinghy because they were afraid the sharp rocks might puncture the raft, and since they were both strong swimmers, they figured it was faster and easier to just swim.

Up close it was easy to tell the panicked creature was in serious trouble. Carefully, they approached it.

The manatee's big sloe eyes were frantic. It floundered, splashed and made a high-pitched, weary squeaking noise like the sound of wiper blades rubbing against a dry windshield. The closer they got the more frantic the mammal's splashing became and the louder and longer its cries grew.

"Easy," Jeb cooed. "Nice and easy, big girl."

"How do you know it's a girl?" Haley asked.

"I don't."

"And here I thought you knew everything there was to know about the sea."

"The sea," he said sagely, "is unknowable."

They had to dog-paddle to reach the stranded mammal. She—Haley was just going to go with the manatee's femininity—stared at them. Her eyes seemed to beg, "Save me."

"We've gotta help her. We can't let this magnificent creature die here."

"Let me see if I can find out what's going on." Jeb dived out of sight and swam underneath the manatee.

"It's okay," Haley soothed. "He knows what he's doing." *I think.*

The manatee looked skeptical.

"I trust him with my life." It was true. She did trust Jeb. More than she'd ever trusted any man besides her father and brother.

Jeb came up, water rolling off his body. He scrubbed a palm down his face, spat out ocean. "Not good."

"What is it?"

"She's got what looks to be bailing wire wrapped all around her. And whenever she moves forward the wire constricts around her. When she relaxes, the wire loosens and she thinks she's free and she surges forward, pulling the wire tight again. No telling how long she's been here. She's pretty exhausted, aren't you, old girl?" A softness lit Jeb's eyes and he tenderly stroked the manatee's back.

Haley's chest tightened. She had given him a hard time, but Jeb had come through with flying colors. He was truly worried about the manatee. "If we could get her to stay relaxed, could we uncoil the wire from around her?"

"Maybe. It would be more efficient to get wire cutters and cut her out, but we need to keep her calm. She could injure herself so easily."

"Where are we going to get wire cutters?"

"I've got some on the yacht."

"I'll stay here with her, see if I can keep her soothed," Haley said. "You go get the wire cutters."

"Are you sure? While manatees are gentle creatures, they're still creatures. She's in pain and distress. No telling what she might do."

"I'll be fine. Go on."

He looked reluctant to leave her. "The water is over your head."

"I can handle myself, Jeb. I know how to float and dog-paddle."

"Okay, but you'll be out here all alone."

"Worry about yourself. You'll be swimming back and forth the entire time."

"Good thing I'm in excellent shape." He grinned, flexed.

"Good thing. Now go."

Chuckling, he swam toward the *Second Chance*. "I'll be back as soon as I can."

Haley's heart crawled into her throat. What a guy. Why had she ever thought him superficial? He was magnificent. Unexpected tears filled her eyes. What was *this?* She blinked, focused her attention on the manatee.

She treaded water beside the mammal and began humming softly. She patted the manatee's thick gray hide and she was surprised to discover she felt just like a wet elephant.

Haley's attention did seem to calm her. The manatee ceased thrashing so hard and just floated. Haley rolled onto her back, floated beside her.

"That's it, sweetie. Just take it easy and Jeb will have you fixed up in no time and you'll be hanging out with other manatees before you know it. That'll be nice, won't it? Just think about that."

Her nursing skills helped her soothe the creature. She thought of Jeb and the effort he was putting forth swimming to the boat and back. She was so proud of him. How she wished she'd gotten to know him better before now. He'd enriched her life in ways she couldn't have imagined. The strains of Phish's "Velvet Sea" pushed through her head and she started humming that song for the manatee, crooning, singing, petting and living in the moment.

She savored the time, pressed it to her chest like a favorite photograph. In the future, if anyone asked her about the defining moments of her life, she'd have to say this sailboat trip, culminating in a manatee rescue, was one of the most life-affirming things she'd ever experienced.

There weren't too many more things in life that could move someone—falling in love, marriage, having a baby. Most people got to do those things, but how many people got to save another living thing? She was so very lucky.

"'Velvet Sea,' huh?" Jeb asked.

Haley startled. She'd been so wrapped up in her thoughts and keeping the manatee quiet that she hadn't heard him swim up. "Phish," she said. "I thought it was appropriate."

"It's one of my favorite ocean songs," he said.

"Mine, too. Not that I have a compilation of seafaring songs or anything."

"I do." He grinned wide. The man was always smiling. "Maybe I'll let you hear my playlist sometime."

When would that be? After tomorrow, she'd never see him again. A sick feeling settled in the pit of her stomach.

"In the meantime," she said, "we have a manatee to save."

Jeb pulled wire cutters from the pocket of his swim trunks. "I'm on the job.

He was. And Haley's cheeks heated. She was terrified he could read the desire in her eyes, so she quickly glanced away.

"Keep up the singing. She's much more relaxed than when we got here. You have a nice singing voice."

Haley stroked the manatee's head, hummed Weezer's "Island in the Sun" while Jeb dived down. He clipped wires and then came back up for air. He would take deep gulps of air and submerge again to clip some more.

She worried about him. While he was in good

shape, that had been quite a swim and it seemed the frequent dipping and cutting was taking a toll. Each time he came up, his face was flushed and his lungs were heaving.

Finally, after a good fifteen minutes, Jeb had cut through enough wire so that the manatee could swing her fin like a paddle.

When he came up for air seconds later, blood was oozing from a cut on his forearm.

Haley gasped softly. "You hurt yourself!"

"Wire got me."

"I'll patch you up when we get back to the boat."

"You spent the whole trip playing nursemaid to me."

"Not the entire trip."

"Okay." He chuckled. "For part of it you played nursemaid to a manatee."

"Hey, what can I say? Birds gotta fly. Fish gotta swim—"

"Haley has to play nurse."

Jeb went below one last time, cut the final wire.

Giddy with freedom, the manatee lunged forward. Haley rocketed back, water filling her nose and her ears, burning her eyes. She came up sputtering, but feeling utterly reborn.

Jeb came along beside her. Together, they watched the manatee swim for open water.

"We did it," she said, pushing wet hair from her eyes. "We saved her."

Jeb touched her shoulder. "Feels good. I'm glad you guilted me into saving her."

"See why I like my job? I get to feel like that almost every day of the week."

"The feeling is hard-won." Wryly, he held up his bleeding arm.

"But worth all the battle scars."

"Yeah." His gazed zeroed in on hers. "It is. That's something I don't think I really realized until now."

"Seriously?"

"You've taught me the value of hard work and sacrifice, Haley."

She arched a skeptical eyebrow. "Are you making fun of me?"

"Not at all." His smile was sweet. "C'mon. Let's go ashore."

They floated toward the rocks, both too exhausted to swim. When the water grew shallow enough, they walked, slogging slowly to shore. Haley's knees were boiled noodles. Her head was stuffy and her skin felt too tight, while at the same time feeling too loose.

The afternoon sun beat down. She squinted her eyes at the *Second Chance,* anchored some distance away, wished for sunglasses and aspirin. She certainly didn't feel up to a twenty-minute swim right now.

Apparently, neither did Jeb. He collapsed, drooping onto his back on a big smooth rock. He lay there, an arm stretched across his flat, taut abs, the muscles in his legs shaking slightly. "That was a hellacious workout."

Haley dropped onto the rock beside him, brought her knees to her chest, rested her chin on her knees.

Jeb's eyes were closed.

She couldn't help staring at him. The man was amazing. Her imagination shifted into hyperdrive. What would it be like to have him inside of her? She yanked her gaze away, looked to where the manatee had disappeared. What was going on with her? Why couldn't she control her wild thoughts?

Nurse mode. Nurse mode always helped.

"Let me see that cut," she said.

He stuck out an arm.

It was a long, straight surface cut. No stitches needed, thankfully. She couldn't do anything for him here anyway. When they got back to the boat, she'd wash it out with antiseptic.

"Give it to me straight, Doc. How bad is it?"

"You'll live."

He opened his eyes, used the palm of his hand to shield his face from the sun. "You ready to swim back?"

"Even if I was, you're not. Your legs are still not steady enough."

"I can handle it." He bounced to his feet, but immediately wobbled. "Wow. Oops."

"You're probably dehydrated. Tell me that you drank some water while you were on board the boat."

He looked chagrined. "I didn't think about it. I was trying to get back here ASAP."

Haley sighed. "Between the sun and the exertion, your body is running on empty."

"I wasn't the only one out there."

A few feet away stood a cluster of palm trees loaded with ripe coconuts. "Coconut water would do the trick. How good are you at cracking open a coconut?" she asked.

"Pretty masterful."

"Coconut cracking in your bag of seduction tricks?"

"You never know when you'll be stranded on a desert island and need a piña colada."

Haley laughed. "I'll get the coconuts. You save your strength for the cracking."

She got up, dusted off her wet bottom and gingerly stepped over the rocks to the sand. At the base of the trees, she found two felled coconuts. She scooped them up and turned to find Jeb behind her.

"Since we're already here and we do need a good rest, why not check out the lighthouse?" She nodded in the direction of the old structure.

"I'm game if you are." He winked.

And damn if this wasn't turning out to be one of the nicest days she'd had in a very long time.

11

Dew point—*The temperature at which the air becomes saturated with water vapor*

AFTER JEB OPENED the coconuts with some expert smashing of hulls against the rocks, they drank the coconut water and ate the fruit. Once their energy returned, they decided to climb to the top of the lighthouse.

Haley's pert fanny swished up the circular stone steps ahead of him. Man alive, she had the finest backside this side of the gulf stream.

Whitcomb, you've got to stop torturing yourself. This is the one that gets away so that the one you're after doesn't. You've spent your entire life flitting from woman to woman. It's time to take a stand and commit. Jackie is the one for you.

So why was the sight of Haley in that pink bikini driving him insane?

She was sexy and he was human. It didn't mean he had to act on it. That was what he'd been telling himself this entire trip. At the top of the stairs lay a wooden landing, and beyond it, the arched opening where lanterns were once hung to warn sailors away from the shallows. History washed over him as he thought about the lives this lighthouse must have saved.

Haley moved to the arched opening, peered out at the landscape below. Jeb came up behind her, his pulse suddenly hammering hard when he caught a scent of her. Even amid the smell of salt and sea and coconut, he could smell her strawberry fragrance. Summer. She smelled like summer. He would never eat strawberries again without thinking about her.

His chest tightened strangely and he wondered what Jackie would have to say about that. Well, he and Jackie needed time to get reacquainted. Obviously, a year apart had changed things, but it wasn't anything that couldn't be put right again.

Yes, and speaking of Jackie, he might have blown everything by agreeing to save that manatee. It was already Friday afternoon and the *Second Chance* was still fifty miles off the coast of Key West. He had the Gulf Stream to navigate, so there was a good chance that he wouldn't make it in time to stop the wedding.

And if that happened? Then what?

Don't panic. You'll make it. Just get the heck out of here now.

He placed a hand on Haley's shoulder to tell her that they needed to go. She turned around, looked deeply into his eyes and smiled a smile so special he felt something in his chest unravel.

Jeb heard mermaids singing, ocean waves crashing, seabirds calling, every bit of it in his head and his heart. From the very moment he'd first laid eyes on Haley, he'd wanted her and fought it. Hard.

But here, now, looking at her, he lost his last shred of control. Jeb leaned in and claimed that pink strawberry mouth for his own.

She let out a soft moan, parted her lips and sank against his chest. Hell, there was only so much a man could take. He cupped her chin in his palm and held her face still while he fully explored that glorious mouth of hers.

She trembled against him. Aroused or scared or both?

He was turned on and scared, too.

They explored each other softly and slowly. When he reluctantly broke the kiss and pulled back, her blue-green eyes had gone murky and she gazed at him with an expression of such desire and confusion he could smell her indecision. Her body tensed in his arms. The blue vein at the hollow of her throat beat rapidly. She wanted to bolt.

And he couldn't blame her. He'd come on too strong. He should not have kissed her.

Even so, he could not resist kissing her again.

The sweet sound of pleasure ripped from her lips cut straight through him, and the next thing he knew she was pulling his head down in a kiss so blistering that if he were to walk buck naked in Antarctica he could not be cooled.

After a long, hard, soul-reaching kiss, she dragged herself away, her chest heaving, her eyes wide and her lips wet with his moisture.

They blinked at each other.

"Again!" she exclaimed.

Laughing, Jeb kissed her a third time. He gently bit her bottom lip and then rolled his tongue over her upper lip. He caressed the small of her back, pressing her tight against him. He kissed her chin, her throat, and he must have found an erogenous zone, since she gasped and clung to him.

"Haley, you taste like heaven."

She laughed nervously, shook her head. Her honey-blond hair tumbled provocatively about her shoulders. He ran two fingers over her cheeks, peered into her eyes, thought of a hundred things he wanted to say. *I want you. I need you. But I can't offer you forever.*

He heard the rumble of thunder, felt the wind blow cool air on their heated skin. He cast a troubled eye to the sky, saw gray clouds gather and bunch.

A storm was coming.

And whether they were ready or not, they were caught in it.

IT WAS FOUR-THIRTY by the time they got back to the boat and the wind was whipping at thirty knots in an easterly direction. Hoping to outrun the impending storm—or at the very least get as close to Key West as he could before the storm hit—Jeb decided to pull in sails and use the engine. He'd run as long as he could, even after dark until the rains came. After that, they'd drop anchor and wait it out. He prayed it would be a swift, quick storm.

Haley helped him secure everything. He was amazed at how much she'd picked up so quickly. He hadn't been exaggerating when he'd called her a natural sailor.

The clouds thickened at sunset, obscuring the sky,

and the air smelled heavily of rain. He kept his eyes on the sky and continued pushing the *Second Chance,* eager to get to Jackie before his feelings for Haley became too much for him to ignore. He was terrified he was falling back into old patterns, becoming easily distracted once he'd made a decision and chosen a course. This was Jeb's personal dead reckoning. His line in the sand. If he turned tail at this point, he feared it meant he would never be able to see anything through to completion.

"Our journey is almost over," Haley said.

"It's been a big adventure. Thank you for taking it with me."

"Jackie's a lucky woman."

He stood at the helm with Haley beside him, coiling up a rope, her eyes downcast. "Haley," he said, "I wish I'd met you at a different time in my life."

"I know."

"Jackie is…" He couldn't finish it. He could tell her how fabulous Jackie was, but she didn't want to hear that. Plus, Haley was just as fabulous in her own way.

This was the crux of his problem. Up until now, he'd been the kind of guy to love the one he was with. He'd fallen into old habits and he was looking at Haley as greener grass. It was his modus operandi, and the only way to break the cycle was not to give in to his desires, but he wanted her in the worst way. Wanted her so badly his bones ached. How was it fate had been so damned fickle as to land Haley here on his boat when he'd been trying to prove a point?

Maybe that was just it. Maybe fate had put her here to test his resolve.

Or maybe, just maybe, fate was trying to tell him that Haley was the one for him and not Jackie.

It was a traitorous thought. One he didn't want to look at too closely. *Everything will work out. Don't worry. Be happy.* Once he saw Jackie and she saw him, all would be resolved.

It sounded good. He'd been dishing up such garbage to himself since he was a kid. But would it really be all right? What if he hurt Haley in the process? It slayed him to think that he might do so.

"I'm going down into the galley," she said, "to make dinner before the storm hits. I'm thinking something simple. Grilled-cheese sandwiches and tomato soup?"

"Sounds good." Food was the last thing on his mind. He was thinking about storms and fate and choices made and desires that could lead you astray and lost loves and, and…

This wasn't like him. He didn't second-guess himself. He made choices, lived with them, moved on.

So stop thinking.

Determinedly, he turned his attention to the sky. The wind was whipping wildly now, the boat rising up on the swells, then roughly slamming back down. The clouds turned an ominous black. He hung with it until the first big splats of rain. Haley appeared at the top of the stairs, motioning him inside. "Come in!" she hollered at him.

She was right. This storm was more powerful than the last one. There would be no sleeping on the bridge for him tonight. Like it or not, he had to go belowdecks and ride out the storm, and he prayed he could weather it without falling into Haley's arms.

THIS WAS HER LAST CHANCE to have a night with Jeb.

He wanted it. She could see it in his eyes, but he was so terribly conflicted. But could she in good conscience seduce him? She wasn't the kind of person who stole another woman's man. Still, she couldn't help dreaming about making love to him.

Stop it. Just stop it.

They ate their meal and did the dishes together, feeling the heat of the storm grow stronger. The sailboat rocked and pitched. They had nothing to do to divert them.

No TV. No computer access. And she wasn't about to play board games with him again. The only thing to do was go to bed and sleep through it.

"You take your bed tonight," she said. "I've hogged it for too long."

"You're fine where you are."

"I'll sleep on the bench seating here."

"Can't. That's where I'll be sleeping."

"Jeb." She shook her head.

"Haley."

What she wanted to do was suggest they share a bed, but of course, she would not do that. "Do you want to shower first?" she asked, "or should I?"

They still hadn't washed the grime of the day off them after rescuing a manatee and climbing a lighthouse and eating coconuts and swimming to the island and back.

"I'll go first," he said. "That way I'll be out of your hair."

While he showered, Haley puttered around the galley kitchen, straightening things that didn't need to be straightened. Her heart felt heavy in her chest and her lungs didn't seem to want to fully inflate. She purposefully drew in several slow, deep, cleansing breaths, and by the time Jeb entered the galley toweling his hair dry and smelling of soap, she had herself under control. Somewhat.

Until he smiled at her.

"I left you plenty of hot water."

"That was nice of you."

He wore pajama bottoms and nothing else. It should be against the law for him to come strutting in here looking so damned available.

Haley pressed two fingers against her lips, remembering what his lips had felt like against hers.

She got up to slip past him, anxious to get to the bathroom for her turn at the shower, but as she went by, the boat lurched, tossing her against him just as the lights went out.

"You okay?" Jeb asked.

"Fine," Haley whispered. She should step away. She was going to step away, but the boat lurched.

The wind howled, picking up speed.

Haley shivered.

"Are you cold?"

No. She was anything but cold.

He stepped forward and rubbed his palms up and down her arms.

She gave in, just gave in and that was all there was to it. She sank against him, as pliable as candle wax.

He pressed his cheek against the top of her head. She could hear the loud, erratic thumping of his heart. Unnerved. He was as unnerved as she was.

Haley licked her lips.

His arms tightened around her.

The boat pitched, tossing them against the furnishings. "We need to sit," he said, "or lie down so that we don't get beat up."

"Yes," she croaked.

"C'mon, I'll guide you to the bedroom."

He took her hand and moved in the darkness. He whacked into something, mumbled a sharp curse. "Didn't need that shin anyway."

His fingers gripped hers gently. "Hold on. Let me take the brunt of the licking."

Licking. Hmm. She'd like to lick him from head to toe.

Haley Jean French! Bite your tongue.

Why did wanting him have to be so wrong? Why couldn't she have met him before he'd taken a vow of celibacy in his attempt to win Jackie? Why couldn't they have met before St. Michael's?

Because before then she would never have considered a torrid affair. She'd been trying to live down her past, trod the straight and narrow, avoid temptation at all costs. And here she'd ended up stuck at sea with the biggest temptation of all.

The rolling and thrusting of the ocean didn't help their progress to the bedroom. The *Second Chance* tossed and floundered one way, then the other. Haley had to admit it was pretty frightening, being out in the ocean with nothing between them and wreckage but a few pieces of wood, fiberglass and metal. She tightened her fingers around his. "Have you ever been in a storm this fierce while on the boat?"

"Yes," he said. "Don't be scared. It'll pass and the sun will come out and everything will be all right."

His optimistic, glass-half-full philosophy was comforting and she wanted to buy it. Oh, how she wanted to buy it. But even if the sun did come out tomorrow and they made it through the night safe and sound, there was always the knowledge that something special had passed her by.

"This way, angel," he crooned.

Angel.

He'd started calling her that the night she'd told him about Trey Goss. The night she'd completely broken down. She'd never told another soul on the face of the earth about what had happened that night, until Jeb. She still didn't know why she'd told him.

After a good five minutes of halting steps, they made it to the cabin. The boat was pitching like a gasoline-powered rocking chair jerking back and forth, back and forth. The rigging creaked and groaned under the onslaught. Lightning flashed. Thunder smashed. She cringed.

"Scared of storms?"

"Not normally, but being out here on the ocean in one makes me feel so vulnerable."

"But it's sort of exhilarating, right?"

In truth, it was.

"More fun than a roller coaster."

"And not nearly as safe," she said.

"Safety is overrated. It keeps you from seizing the day."

"Seize a live wire and you can end up electrocuted."

"Touché."

Wasn't that exactly what she'd done with Jeb? Seized a live wire?

A flash of lightning through the porthole lit up the cabin in a momentary flash of brilliant white light.

In a freeze-frame strobe, she saw Jeb's face and on it was an expression of total male desire combined with a sweet sense of awe and wonder as he looked at her.

"Here are your accommodations for the night, angel," he said, putting a hand around her waist and guiding her to the bed.

She stood beside him, her fingers laced through his. They were breathing in tandem. The storm shook, shouted.

The waves smacked against the boat with even more force than before. The *Second Chance* listed hard starboard, throwing Haley down onto the bed and Jeb on top of her.

His pelvis was pressed against her, his erection hard against her thigh.

"I'm sorry," he apologized.

"Hey," she whispered, "it happens."

"Not like this. Not like it does with you."

Her face flushed and she was grateful for the darkness.

He moved to get up, but the boat pitched again, throwing him right back down on top of her.

"Hang on," he said. "I'll make my getaway in the lull of the next wave."

It sounded good, but when he tried to get up again, the same thing happened.

"Looks like you're stuck here until the storm calms down."

"Just until the worst of it passes," he said.

"I'll just lie right here against the wall." She scooted over. "And you can stay right there on the outside."

"Good plan."

"Let's imagine an invisible line running right down the middle of the bed."

"Me on my side, you on yours."

"Exactly."

"No crossing."

"None."

"You don't touch me, I won't touch you."

"Deal."

"This won't be a problem. None at all."

"Nope. Easy peasy. We can share a bed without anything happening."

"We're adults."

"Fully in control of ourselves."

"Absolutely."

The silence lasted for almost a minute.

"Haley," he breathed in the darkness.

That was all it took. That husky whisper and she crossed that invisible line of restraint she'd had a tenuous hold on since the beginning of the trip. He was waiting for her, arms outstretched. His lips captured hers and he was kissing her with a hunger that stole all the air from her lungs.

The muscles deep in her feminine core clenched and released in a startlingly strong rhythm—aching, begging, craving. In a mad frenzy, they ripped off each other's clothing as the ship bucked and rolled. Thunder and lightning set the mood, rough and electric.

Jeb's mouth was hot against her breast, his wicked tongue challenging her nerve endings, a scrumptious threat. His body was stretched the length of hers, Haley's back pressed into the mattress. His erection a steel rod between them.

Her heart pounded so loudly in her ears she couldn't

hear anything else. She was lost at sea, storm-tossed and loving it.

Supporting his weight on his forearms, he hovered above her, his palms pressed on either side of her face. A flash of lightning illuminated his dear face. He stared into her eyes, his expression one of pure awe, pinning her to the spot.

A lump of emotion clogged her throat. She shouldn't be doing this. It couldn't lead anywhere, but maybe that was exactly why she should do it. Just throw out the rule book and let nature take its course. She was a nurse. She understood biological needs. It didn't have to mean anything more than that.

Sure. That was her plan. Just enjoy the physical and block out the mental and emotional. So what if her heart gave a wistful twist when the corner of his mouth lifted in a boyish quirk? A special smile meant just for her.

He moved his hands from her face; inquisitive fingers explored her body. At his touch, her breasts swelled and her nipples stood erect. His mouth played with her nipples, teased first one and then the other.

She moaned and threaded her fingers through his hair, encouraging him to keep doing the lovely things he was doing. Losing control, she tightened her grip on his hair.

A ragged chuckle rolled from his throat. "Let's see if we can make you do more of that," he murmured against her navel, the sound vibrating clear to her spine.

Yes.

Up they went on the ocean swells, the boat lurching, the waves pummeling an onslaught of sensation through their bodies.

He kissed her cheeks, her neck, and she came completely unraveled, her body clenching and releasing in widening waves. She drew in short, rapid breaths of air, savored the smell of this masculine man doing wondrous things to her.

As fun as it was to let him steer the course, Haley believed in an equal partnership. While his mouth and tongue did crazy things to her, she reached a hand down and stroked the velvet tip of his manhood poking against her thigh.

He let loose an appreciative groan and slid down the flat of her belly, his tongue licking and swirling, stoking her arousal. Finally, he raised his head, hair sticking every which way from where she'd mussed it, and he flashed her the most beguiling grin.

She smiled back at him, enchanted.

Gracefully, he leaned forward, his chest puffing up like a spinnaker filling with wind. "Hang on, angel, we're going body sailing."

"What?" she asked, a bit confused, but he answered her question with his body instead of words.

His fingers trailed from her waist, down the flat of her belly to the curve of her hip, and then traveled around her thigh until he found her most intimate spot. She exhaled on a sigh, every muscle in her body liquefied.

"I want to make love to you so badly I can taste it."

His declaration stirred her. She wanted him, too. She touched him again, letting him know it was full speed ahead, cupping the weight of his masculinity in her palm.

"You're so sexy," he crooned. "Haley, I can't believe you're even here with me."

She couldn't believe it, either.

He paused a moment, looked down into her face again. "Are you sure this is what you want?"

"Yes." She whimpered, unable to bear the thought of not having his body joined with hers. Only he could quench the fire burning inside her. Only he had the key to her lock. "More than anything!"

He reached for something in the overhead compartment and pulled out a condom. Ever ready for a sea adventure. Some nurse she was. So overcome by desire she'd forgotten about protection. Thankfully, Jeb was thinking. He tore open the packet with his teeth.

"Let me," she said, taking the condom from him and rolling it on the length of his throbbing, hot erection. When she finished, they were both breathing hard and desperate.

"Put your legs on my shoulders," he urged.

She obeyed. The position raised her hips up off the mattress. He was between her legs, the head of his shaft poised at her entrance. He was quivering, as excited as she.

Haley arched her back, tipped her butt down and stared up into his eyes. "I want you."

"I want you," he whispered.

Unable to resist another second, she brought his head down to hers for a long, heartfelt kiss.

He eased his body into hers—tender and loving. How good it felt. She closed her eyes, floating on the absolute bliss of the moment.

The timbers were shivering, along with everything

else on the boat. While the storm raged fiercely outside, their passion raged even fiercer inside the cabin.

Jeb moved slowly, letting her get accustomed to him and she whispered her approval, used her legs to draw him more deeply inside of her.

"You are so tight," he murmured. "Beautiful."

She squeezed him with her internal muscles and he groaned. She slipped her hands around his forearms, holding on for the thrill ride of her life. How was it she'd lived so long without knowing sex could feel like this? Innocent. She felt like an innocent experiencing sex for the first time.

"I feel like a virgin," she whispered, "with you."

"Me, too," he said with such sincerity that she almost believed him.

Over the course of the past few days, he'd taught her a lot about taking life as it came instead of always fighting against the current.

Certainly being with him was light, easy. All she had to do was relax into him. Have fun. He was so much fun to be with. He made everything a game. He opened her eyes to so many possibilities. In his presence, life was an exciting adventure waiting to be explored.

And right now, all kinds of heady feelings were flowing through her.

"Everything about you is intense, isn't it?" he crooned.

It was true. She came at life as if it was a battle to be won.

"Okay, that's the way we'll do this. Here we go, angel," he murmured, his voice raw and strained. "Overboard."

She thrust upward just as he thrust down, meeting him halfway, pushing and rubbing, caressing and stroking, until their bodies beaded with perspiration. Friction.

They were a craze of arms and legs, mouths and teeth and tongues. After a few desperate minutes, he changed the tempo, slowing down, dragging it out.

Haley whimpered with frustration.

"Let's make it last," he explained.

Oh.

He tightened his buttocks, eased out of her.

She whimpered louder.

He gave a self-satisfied laugh.

"Tease," she mumbled.

"A good tease never hurt anyone."

She rolled over onto her hands and knees, wriggled her fanny, and he let out a groan. "Ha, not so cocky now, huh?"

"I'm plenty cocky. We're just getting started."

"Promises, promises."

"Now who's being cocky?" He lightly swatted her fanny.

"Punishing me?"

"Never. This is all about your pleasure."

Her insides clenched hard and she was panting. "Do it again," she whispered.

"This?" His palm cupped her fanny again, gave her a short little smack.

Blood shot through her veins, rushing adrenaline to her heart.

"You like this?"

Mutely, she nodded. She wasn't sure how far she wanted it to go, but right now, her pulse sprinted like a racehorse and her entire body hammered with excitement.

Another quick swat.

They were all alone out here. Just her and Jeb and the ocean and the storm, but she trusted him completely. That surprised her most of all. She didn't trust easily, but somehow, she knew deep down inside that Jeb would never hurt her. Maybe that was why she felt so free to whisper her secret spanking fantasy into his ear. She wanted him more than she'd ever wanted anything in her life.

"Please," she whispered, without even knowing for sure what she was begging for. "Please."

He cupped her buttocks in his palms.

She buried her face into the pillow and he gently entered her again. Overjoyed, she wanted to sing.

"Haley," he called her name, and the sound of it pouring from his lips did strange and wondrous things to her.

Playful. Their coupling was playful and lighthearted, and in this sweet game, they found their release together, as their ecstatic cries were drowned out by the snarling storm.

12

Ebb—*A tidal current flowing out to sea*

"Now," Jeb said, "we're going to do it my way."

"Mmm," Haley murmured, reached up to trace an index finger over his bottom lip. "How is that?"

"Slow and sweet and I want you on your back so I can see your face."

"Why, Jeb Whitcomb, you're a traditionalist at heart. Who knew?"

Outside, the storm was ebbing, the lightning a weak flutter from distant clouds, thunder a muted grumble, but inside, Jeb was in tumult. He couldn't keep his hands off Haley. Couldn't think of anything but making love to her again, but in just a few hours, weather willing, they'd be hitting land in Florida.

And then what?

His chest tightened and his skin prickled.

Haley tangled her fingers in the hairs at his chest and her gentle tickling drove him wild. He closed his eyes, took in a deep breath, tried to grasp some small shred of control.

Haley.

She kissed from his chest to his belly, going to a place he longed for her to go, but didn't want to ask. A groan, half pleasure, half despair, slipped past his lips. There was no stopping now. He'd already sped past the point of no return. The woman had reduced him to rubble.

Her sweet lips touched the head of his shaft and it was all he could do not to lose it instantly. She took charge, closing her mouth around him.

Ah, hell, he'd wanted to make love to her face-to-face, look deeply into her eyes, but if she kept going the way she was going, he'd be spent before they got that far.

He tried to pull her back up, but she resisted, her tongue doing startling things to him. He grasped her hair in his fists, tugging gently. "Angel, I want to be inside you."

She give a wicked laugh and did a little maneuver that sent him over the edge. Without warning the orgasm overtook him.

Haley.

Clenching his jaw, he shuddered as he climaxed, shaking and chanting her name.

When it was over, she collapsed onto the bed beside him. "Turnabout is fair play." She laughed.

He could hear his own heart beat, taste the black, mysterious shadows of the darkened room. He inhaled it—the night—smelling thickly of their lovemaking and the ozone scent from discharged lightning.

Haley.

The sexy woman who challenged him to be a better man. The woman who'd captured his heart. He gathered her to him, hugged her close and kissed the top of her head.

They slumbered like that for a while, then he woke her sometime later with more kisses, got another condom from the cabinet and finally made love to her the way he'd ached to make love to her for months.

Face-to-face. Eye to eye. Just the two of them, in the quiet, reverent lull left by the vanishing storm.

WHAT HAD SHE DONE?

Haley lay in bed beside a sleeping Jeb, the sheet wrapped around her waist, staring up at the ceiling as tendrils of dawn blushed pink about the porthole. She looked over at him. The man was so handsome and for a second she forgot everything except how glorious it felt to be next to him.

Wonder how many other women have been in this same spot.

That made her stomach hurt.

She hitched in her breath, returned her gaze to the ceiling. See. That was what was wrong with this scenario, as nice—oh, who was she kidding, it had been incredible—as last night had been, he pined for this Jackie woman.

That was the thing. She would not romanticize what had happened between her and Jeb. The storm has tossed them into bed together and they simply hadn't been able to keep their hands off each other. Proximity and sexual chemistry equaled heady lust, *not* true love.

So why did it hurt so much?

She couldn't stop herself from peeping over at him again. His generous mouth was relaxed, welcoming. His square jaw was scruffy with a sandy-colored beard, and a lock of hair flopped boyishly over his forehead. Even when he was asleep, he was fun-loving. Really, it was better that they were going their separate ways. They didn't fit together. Honestly, what did they have in common?

Oreos. Double-stuffed. Kept in the refrigerator.

Cold Oreos were not enough to base a relationship on.

As if he was even considering a relationship with you. Stop hoping. There's no hope. Snuff it out. You can't dare let him know that you're hoping for something he can't deliver. It will just make both of you feel bad.

Besides, she'd violated her own code of ethics, making love to a man whose heart belonged to another woman. She deserved this. She'd known better and she'd allowed it to happen anyway.

Misery ate at her.

There was no other way to handle this than to pretend last night had meant absolutely nothing more than scratching an itch. He would be relieved that she had no expectations from him. When they made land in Florida, he'd go to Jackie, she'd return home to St. Michael's.

It was the only way to deal with the situation—deny her feelings. What were feelings anyway but fleeting emotions subject to change? It was the sensible solution and it would protect her from a mountain of hurt.

Her mind made up about the strategy to take, she turned over on her stomach and stuffed the corner of the pillow into her mouth so Jeb could not hear her sobs.

THE WIND WAS LIGHT and from the south, making crossing the Gulf Stream into Key West easier than usual. With this early start and the calm after the storm, they could just sail right in. He had an open channel straight to Jackie.

Fate had spoken. Even with going through customs and taking Haley to the airport to catch a charter plane back to St. Michael's, he would have plenty of time to stop Jackie's wedding.

Except, now he did not know if he wanted to do that.

Jackie seemed so far away, part of another life.

What was real, what was genuine, was the woman standing on the bridge beside him.

Haley.

He cut his eyes over at her.

She seemed so peaceful. A week ago if someone had told him she'd be on his boat and that they would make love and she'd seem so calm about it afterward, he would have laughed. It was an image he couldn't have dreamed of.

This morning, she'd gotten up and made breakfast and greeted him with a cheery smile when he'd stumbled from the cabin, but when he'd tried to catch her around the waist and give her a kiss, she'd slipped away from him. Her shoulders stiffened and her smile faltered.

Uh-oh. She was giving him the morning-after brush-off. He knew because he'd used it on women, and he knew with absolutely certainty that if they'd been on dry land, she would have taken off in the middle of the night.

The woman had turned the tables on him, giving him a dose of his own roguish behavior.

Except he'd been trying so hard to change. Wanted desperately to redeem himself.

Maybe Haley was the instrument of his final redemption. Even though he'd given in to last night's wild temptation, he was feeling firsthand what it was like to be used for sex.

The old Jeb would have lapped it up, but this new Jeb was ashamed to think he'd ever made others feel the way he was feeling now.

Taken advantage of.

"Last night—"

"Is over," Haley said brightly and shoved a cup of coffee into his hand. "I had fun, but there's no need to dissect it. Things got out of hand and we crossed a line, but there's no need to feel guilty or ashamed. I release you from any sense of obligation you might be feeling toward me."

"I…I…" He was speechless.

"We should get going," she said, "if you intend on breaking up a wedding."

She'd walked away, gone topside, leaving him with nothing to do but scoot after her.

Jeb didn't erect the sails, but instead powered up the engines for the ride into Key West.

Haley moved port side, sat down, looked out to sea, her honey-colored hair glistening in the dawn. She looked completely unaffected by what they'd shared last night and her cavalier attitude was a punch in the gut.

She doesn't care. You should be happy about that. You have a goal, a plan, and Haley isn't part of it.

Jackie. That was where his future lay.

Why, then, did his chest tighten and a sick feeling rise in his throat?

Why? He'd let Jackie down, he'd let Haley down, but most of all he'd let himself down.

That was the core of it. He'd wanted to prove to Haley that he was an honorable, ethical man. Her high standards had made him want to raise his expectations of himself, but he'd failed. Big-time.

He navigated the boat, but his mind wasn't on sailing; it was tangled up around Haley, as tight as fishing line. She must have sensed he was staring at her because she swiveled purposely and met his gaze, gave him a brief smile.

His heart capsized.

He had a hundred things he wanted to say to her, but didn't know how to start. *Thank you for the gift of last night. I'm sorry if I've caused you pain in any way. I'll miss you.*

She glanced away.

What was she thinking? He couldn't get a read on her. Which was odd. Normally, with Haley you knew exactly where you stood.

He opened his mouth; shut it. He donned his sunglasses.

She reached into the storage compartment where he kept supplies, took out a bottle of sunblock and squeezed some into her palm.

Not gonna watch her. Not gonna do it.

Jeb tilted his head, slid her a sideways glance.

Haley slathered the lotion over her tanned arms.

Moisture filled his mouth. He licked his lips. Swallowed hard.

Her long fingers massaged the lotion into her skin in slow, rhythmic circles.

He hardened instantly. This was bad.

Haley stretched out one long, shapely leg, rubbed it with a fresh squirt of lotion.

Sweat popped out on Jeb's brow. He blew out his breath and yanked his gaze away. *Drive the damn boat.* He clenched his jaw, did his best to think of Jackie and steered the *Second Chance* toward Key West.

HALEY SMILED AND SMILED and smiled, but it was all an act.

Inside, her heart was aching and nausea settled low in her stomach. Last night, she'd thrown caution to the wind and allowed her body to dictate her behavior. Mistake. Huge mistake. And why was she shocked?

She'd asked for this, but she hadn't expected just how much it would hurt to walk away.

The wind whipped her hair against her face and she kept her eyes glued toward the sea. She would be okay. She would survive this. She was tough.

A tear slid down her cheek. Quickly, she scrubbed it away. None of that nonsense. She'd cried all she was going to cry over him.

She drew her knees to her chest, smelled Jeb's scent on the T-shirt she wore thrown over the pink bikini. There was no escaping him. Not while she was on this boat.

Land lay ahead. Soon, her adventure would be over.

Jeb navigated the Gulf Stream like a hot knife slicing through cold butter. Haley couldn't help sneaking surreptitious glances at him. The wind blew his hair back off his handsome face, and his sturdy fingers gripped the wheel. Fingers that just a few short hours ago had been igniting her body in a hundred different ways.

He caught her eye and she quickly glanced away, feigned nonchalance, dipped her shoulder down and stroked the polished wood with her big toe. She missed the sails, how they would billow out wide in the breeze. Missed the sound of the rigging banging against the mast. Motoring into port instead of gracefully sailing in on the wind felt like defeat.

She was going to be okay. It was not the end of the world. Never mind that she was a wrung-out dishrag and her bones were made of rubber. She'd put one foot in front of the other, move through this, past this.

Key. Jeb had given her the key to a new way of being. She could relax and let go. She didn't always have to be in control, and that was a good thing. She was grateful for the gift he'd given her and she would treasure it forever, even if a hole gaped in the middle of her heart.

13

Death roll—*A capsize to windward; generally occurs while sailing downwind*

THREE HOURS LATER, they made it through customs in Key West. Jeb rented a white convertible and drove her to the airport, where he chartered a plane for her.

"Well," he said, as they stood in the reception area of Island Conch Charters, other passengers going to and fro, "I guess this is goodbye."

"It's been an experience I'll never forget."

Their gazes met. The tender look in his eyes held her and a bittersweet smile played at the corners of his mouth.

Outside the window, lightning flashed so close it sizzled brilliantly bright across the sky, immediately followed by a loud clash of thunder. Unnerved, Haley jumped. The ramp crew came running into the building, signaled to the receptionist, who got on the PA address system and announced that the ramp would be closed until the lightning passed.

"Looks like I've got a wait," she said, smoothing

wrinkles from the skirt of the little blue flowered dress she'd worn on board Jeb's ship six days ago. She'd changed so much in such a short amount of time.

Jeb guided her toward a leather couch in the lobby, sat down with her. She wished he'd just leave.

"I want to thank you, Haley," he murmured.

"For what?"

"Making my life richer."

If she'd made his life so rich, why was he running off after another woman? "You're the one who's enriched my life."

He reached out to take her hand.

She wanted to resist, pull back. She should have, but instead, she sank against him.

"I'm going to miss you."

"Ditto." She could barely push the word past her constricted throat.

"I want to write to you—"

She shook her head. "No."

"Just as friends."

"No." She stepped away from him.

He jammed his hands in his pockets, rounded his shoulders. "I know."

If only they could be friends! But he'd given his heart to another woman, and Haley was not going to come between them. She'd already crossed a line that she should not have crossed. She refused to compound an error in judgment by encouraging him.

"You should go," she said coolly.

"Haley—"

"I mean it. Just go." She jerked her head away, blinking rapidly to banish the tears collecting behind her eyelids.

"You're very special to me," he said. "I'd rather cut off my arm than hurt you. I never intended for any of this to happen. You've got to believe me."

Here was the issue. She *did* believe him, but it didn't change a darn thing.

He reached for her again.

This time, she was strong enough to ward him off. She held up her palm. Stop sign. "I know you didn't mean to hurt me."

"But I did," he whispered.

She wasn't about to give him that kind of power over her feelings. "I'm fine, Jeb. You didn't hurt me. Not in the least."

He looked hurt, then relieved and then suspicious. "You're just saying that to spare me."

"Honestly," she lied through her teeth, "I'm not shattered."

A sheepish expression crossed his face. "I like you, Haley. I like you a great deal."

"I like you, too, but that doesn't matter, does it?"

"What do you mean?"

"C'mon, even if you weren't on the way to stop your ex-girlfriend from marrying someone else, you and me..." She toggled a finger between them, shook her head. "We don't belong together, but you and Jackie Birchard? Now, that's a match made in high-society heaven. You're both rich, accustomed to fame and move in the same circles. You're both seafaring folks. You speak the same language. You and me? We're like hot dogs and caviar."

"Hey, you took to the sea like an otter."

Haley traced his face with her gaze. He was the epitome of a wealthy yachtsman and she carried bedpans for a living. No matter how she might try to convince herself otherwise, she would not fit into his world. "It was fun for a while, but you can't raise kids on the sea, and that's what I want one day—a husband, kids, an ordinary life. Let's face it. You're too extraordinary for me, Jeb Whitcomb."

"You're the extraordinary one, Haley French, and I'm the one who's not good enough for you."

"While we had a good time in bed, there's a big difference between heating up the sheets and being good together as a couple."

He sucked in his breath through clenched teeth and his color paled beneath his tan. "Yeah," he mumbled. "You're probably right."

"I *am* right."

"I wish—"

"No sense wishing things to be different. They are what they are." She forced a smile.

"Haley, I—"

Broken, she swallowed hard. "You better go or you'll be too late to stop the wedding."

"What if I were?" he said softly.

She pretended she hadn't heard him, stood up, turned away, because if she didn't, she was terrified that she would get down on her knees and plead with him to stay.

It was 3:45 p.m.

With fifteen minutes to spare, Jeb drove into the Wharf 16 parking lot where Jackie's wedding was being held aboard the *Sea Anemone,* his mind glazed with sweet thoughts of Haley.

He sat in the rental car, picked up his cell to dial

her number. Put it down. Picked it up again and then realized he didn't even know her cell-phone number. How could he be crazy for a woman when he didn't even know her cell-phone number?

Um, how can you be crazy for her when you're here to tell Jackie that you love her?

That was just the thing, wasn't it?

He switched off the phone, watched the digital clock flip to 3:47. Wedding guests walked passed him on their way to the *Sea Anemone*. Wedding music swelled in the air—the Carpenters, of all things. That sounded too romantic and cheesy for Jackie.

Why wasn't he jumping out of the car, running up the gangplank, demanding that they stop the wedding? Protesting that he was speaking now instead of forever holding his peace?

He drummed his fingers on the steering wheel, felt his throat tighten. Haley had said that a seafaring lifestyle wasn't for her, but he'd seen the way she'd looked when she'd spied those dolphins—free, alive, *happy*. She said she wanted to get married and have kids some day, and for the first time in his life, Jeb realized he wanted that, too.

A car with a U-Haul trailer towed behind it pulled into the parking lot behind Jeb. A tall man in his early thirties wearing a leg brace got out of the passenger seat and hobbled toward the ship. Jeb recognized the man as Jackie's older half brother, Boone, but he didn't call out to the former Iraq war vet. Boone looked to be a man on a mission, his face set into a dark frown.

Jeb knew that he and Jackie had a lot in common— divorced parents, half siblings, money, their love of the sea. They would be perfect together.

Except whenever Jeb closed his eyes, Jackie was not the blonde he saw. Rather it was Haley's honey-colored hair that clouded his vision, Haley who made his blood pound.

Boone talked to an usher at the gangplank, went over to a building on the pier. It was now 3:50 and still, Jeb sat there.

Jackie and Boone came out of the building together. They were having a serious discussion. Jackie wore an elegant white dress and looked drop-dead gorgeous.

Jeb felt…well, hell, he felt nothing except happiness for her.

No desire. No sexual attraction. No burning need. No desperation.

Instead, he thought of Haley.

He could not say why he was so drawn to her. Sure, she was pretty, but he'd been with more beautiful women—Jackie was a case in point. Maybe it was because Haley had disliked him and he couldn't stand for people not to like him. In the beginning, he'd done everything he could to impress her, and the harder he'd tried, the less impressed she'd been. It had only been when he'd stopped trying so hard that he'd begun to win her over.

He thought of the fun they'd had—sailing, spotting dolphins, playing drinking games, saving a manatee, exploring a lighthouse.

Making love.

A rap sounded against the window and Jeb startled.

There was Jackie with the biggest grin on her face. She wrenched open the door. "Jeb!"

He got out and she folded him in an enthusiastic hug.

"I'm so happy you made it. You're here and Boone

showed up with his girl. My two favorite men in the whole world—besides Scotty, of course." Jackie blushed prettily.

Never, in all the years that he'd known her, had Jeb ever seen Jackie blush.

"We're holding up the wedding a few minutes so Boone and his girl can join us." Jackie held out her arms as if she wanted to embrace the whole world. "And now that you're here, too, my wedding day is complete."

"Jackie, I..." *This is it. The part where you tell her that you love her and that you don't want her to marry this Scott character.*

"Yes?" Her smile was as bright as the sun.

Jeb swallowed, a little stunned. "I'm happy for you."

It was true. He was happy for her.

Jackie linked her arm through his and tugged him toward the *Sea Anemone*. Dazed, he simply let her. He wasn't in love with Jackie. He never had been. Not in a romantic sense. He'd admired and respected her and they were friends, but he'd never felt for Jackie what he felt for Haley.

"What is it?" Jackie asked. "What's wrong?"

He told her everything.

"You came here to bust up my wedding?"

"Yes, but I no longer want to do that. I can tell from your face that you're madly in love with Scott."

"I am," she said with such conviction it bowled him over. "Now, tell me about Haley."

He smiled big. "She's the most amazing woman I've ever known."

"You're in love with her."

"Yeah," he admitted.

"So what's the problem?"

He shook his head. "She doesn't love me."

Jackie sighed and shook her head. "Men. You're impossible."

"In what way?"

"You told her you were coming here to stop my wedding, right?"

Mutely, he nodded.

"She thinks you're madly in love with me. She thinks you're making this grand romantic gesture."

"I was going to—"

"But somewhere along the way you fell in love with her."

"I did."

"But you were afraid that if you let yourself show how you felt about her that it would mean I was right about you when I accused you of being a fickle play-boy who only wanted what he couldn't have."

"Yeah." He ducked his head, splayed his palm to the nape of his neck.

"Well, think about it from her point of view. If she's in love with you, she's certainly not going to admit it when she believes that you're either in love with an-other woman or a fickle playboy."

Jackie had a point.

"You think…" He paused, his heart pounding. Could it be true? Could Haley be in love with him? He was scared to hope.

"I think."

"What should I do?"

"Tell her how you feel."

Jeb clenched his jaw.

"Don't let fear hold you back. I know you've had commitment issues in the past—"

"It's not a commitment issue," he said. "I want Haley more than I've ever wanted anything in my life. I'm just trying to decide if I should drive to the airport before she takes off or if I should stay here for the wedding."

Jackie pointed to the car. "Go."

"And if she's already gone?"

"You catch the next plane and go after her."

He looked into his friend's eyes. Jackie was truly a good friend. "You don't mind?"

"I'll bean you over the head if you don't go. I had to learn the hard way, Jeb. When you find someone who loves you inside and out, for all your strengths and flaws, don't ever let them go."

14

Fetch—*The distance of open water that waves have to grow*

JEB RACED TO THE AIRFIELD in the rental car, pushing it past the limit and praying he didn't get pulled over for speeding. Could he convince Haley to forgive him? He'd been so dumb. So blind to what was right in front of him.

He'd dumped her off at the airport so he could go off to chase after another woman. Fool. He'd treated her cruelly. After the way he'd acted, he didn't deserve a second chance, didn't deserve to even beg for her forgiveness.

But he had to try. He could not let her slip through his fingers.

What if the plane had already left? It had probably already left, even with the weather delay.

Well, if the plane had already left, he'd get another plane and fly to St. Michael's after her, but he hoped it hadn't left. He couldn't wait to touch her again, even though it had only been a few hours. Kiss her again. Tell her that he loved her.

Because he loved her with a fierceness that took his breath away.

It would serve him right if she wouldn't forgive him. His stomach clenched and his hands froze on the steering wheel. No. He could not afford to think like that. She would forgive him. He *had* to convince her. Winning her love was the most important mission of his life.

The *only* mission of his life that really mattered, because without Haley, he was only half the man he could be.

Pulse racing, he darted into the airport parking lot. Jeb jumped from the car, rushed through the building of the fixed-based operator. "The charter flight to St. Michael's," he hollered at the receptionist. "Is it still here?"

"They're just about to take off."

He raced for the ramp door marked Employees Only.

"Sir! Sir!" The receptionist jumped to her feet. "You can't go out there. The plane is about to taxi out. Sir! If you go on the ramp, I'm calling security."

"STOP THE PLANE!"

Haley raised her head and glanced out the window of the small charter jet.

Jeb came running up, waving his arms at the pilot in the cockpit. "Stop the plane!"

"Who the hell is this joker?" the pilot asked the copilot through the open door of the cockpit as they completed their flight checks.

Heart in her throat, Haley sprang to her feet. "He's with me. Don't take off."

"Kill the engines," the pilot told the copilot.

Haley ran to the door, fumbled for the latch. "How do you open this thing?"

"Hang on." The copilot came to her rescue. "What's going on?"

"I don't know," Haley said, but she hoped, oh, how she hoped, that this was her second chance.

The door opened, and with it, automatic stairs came down.

Haley flew down the steps just as Jeb scaled up them. They met in the middle and their eyes hooked on each other.

Could it be...? She had no clue why he'd come to stop her from taking off, but she couldn't help hoping that he was here to grovel.

"What is it?" she asked. "Jackie turned you down so you came to claim second place with me?"

"No," he said. "I came to apologize for being the world's biggest idiot."

Her heart pumped blood through her ears so loudly she wasn't sure she heard him. Her chest squeezed and she felt faintly dizzy. "You can be pretty clueless," she conceded.

"Not anymore," he said.

"About Jackie?"

"About you."

"About me?" she whispered.

"You're the one that I want. The only one I need."

"You expect me to take that to the bank?"

"Haley." He looked miserable, threaded a hand through his hair. "It kills me to think I've hurt you."

"The only way you'll hurt me is if you don't truly mean the stuff you're saying."

Jeb sank to his knees on the step below her, clasped his hands together in a pleading gesture. "Haley French, I've never in my life professed my love to another woman."

Love! Her heart leaped. "Not even to your mother or your sisters?"

"You know what I mean. Pay attention."

"Not even to Jackie?"

"No."

"Not even when you got to the wedding?"

"No, because I realized that while I do love Jackie—"

Haley inhaled audibly, splayed a palm to her chest, felt her heart stumble.

"—I don't *love* her, love her. I love her as a friend and *nothing more*. That's where I kept getting tangled up. I had feelings for Jackie, but I didn't understand that those were feelings of friendship, not romantic love."

Haley folded her arms over her chest. "It sure took you a long time to figure that out."

"Not really," he said. "It just took me a long time to admit it. I've been falling for you since that sunset on Diver's Beach. I was just too scared to admit it, too afraid I was simply falling into an old, familiar pattern of hopping from one woman to the next as soon as things got serious."

"How do you know you're not doing that now?"

"Because I've never met anyone like you. Never felt like this."

"I'm not convinced," she said, ignoring her wildly fluttering heart. How she wanted to believe him!

"I named my boat the *Second Chance*."

"Because of another woman."

"Jackie might have set me on my journey," he said, "but the journey led me to you."

"Uh-huh." She was trying desperately to be cool when all she wanted to do was fling herself into his arms and kiss him until their lips were raw.

"Haley, I know I'm asking you to overlook a lot of things—"

"Like the fact that you're a womanizer."

"Was. That's firmly in the past."

"How do I know that you won't change your mind?"

"I've never told a woman that I loved her before. Not in a romantic way. For all my faults, I've never thrown that word around to get someone into bed. Love means something to me."

"Not even Jackie?"

"Not even Jackie. You're it, Haley. My one and only. I love you."

Haley moistened her lips. "Jeb."

Fear flared in his eyes as if an incomprehensible thought had just speared his brain. "Oh," he said, looking completely stricken, "you don't love *me*."

She couldn't keep torturing him this way. "Silly man, of course I love you."

"How's a guy supposed to know that? Especially when you went out of your way to tell me how wrong I was for you."

"I was trying to protect myself."

"But you love me." A grin kidnapped his entire face.

"I do."

He pulled her into his arms right there on the steps of the airplane and kissed her soundly. He took his time, his tongue leisurely coaxing and teasing.

"Okay," she said, breaking the kiss with a reluctant sigh, "we need to get something straight."

"I'm all ears."

She met sumptuous eyes the color of the sea. "I'm not the easiest person to get along with."

"Uh-huh." He leaned in to nibble her earlobe.

Haley's pulse skittered. "I have strong convictions."

"Don't worry, I know how to get you to relax."

He certainly did at that. He'd taught her that it was okay to enjoy herself once in awhile. That life didn't have to be a grim proposition filled with responsibilities and expectations.

"I have a tendency to judge first and give second chances grudgingly."

"I know." His fingers kneaded her shoulders.

"I'd had a bad experience with a wealthy man. I lumped you in the same category, but you fooled me."

"You're admitting you were wrong?"

"Don't get smug about it. You've got a few flaws yourself."

"Who, me?" He kissed the tip of her nose.

"You are given to grand gestures, like running up and trying to stop a plane."

"Guilty as charged."

"Not a smart thing to do."

"It worked, didn't it?" He tickled her lightly in the ribs and she chuckled. "But you were right about me. I was a cocky guy used to getting my way and being adored."

"I didn't think—"

"You did and you were right, but thanks to you—"

"And Jackie—she's the one who gave you the shove you needed to come to St. Michael's in the first place. I owe her a thank-you gift."

"I'm just grateful that I recognized how I felt about you. Honestly, I think it happened the day you got hit by the boom."

"And you kissed the breath back into me."

He peered into her eyes, held her tightly in his arms. "And I want to keep doing it for the rest of our lives."

What romantic words! They struck her heart like an arrow from a quiver. "For me," she said, "that night we played I've Never and I told you about my secret shame and you didn't judge or condemn me for it. In fact, you comforted me, held me in your arms. That was the night I knew it was more than sex or infatuation."

"But the sex is good, right?" He wriggled his eyebrows.

"Not even close."

"No?" He looked so crestfallen, she almost laughed out loud.

"It's the most amazing sex I've ever had."

"For me, too." He winked. "And that's saying something."

Playfully, she swatted his upper arm.

"What say we let these pilots have their plane back and head back to the *Second Chance*?"

"Under one condition," Haley said.

"What's that?"

"We change the name of that boat."

"Haven't you heard? It's bad luck to change the name of the boat."

"You changed it before and very good luck came your way. You're not superstitious, are you?"

"Not when I'm with you. What should we change the name to?"

"How about the *Happily Ever After?*"

"Exactly what I was thinking."

He took her into his arms once more, kissed her hard and long and sweet until Haley knew in her heart that from here on out, everything between them would be smooth sailing.

* * * * *

REQUEST YOUR FREE BOOKS!
2 FREE NOVELS PLUS 2 FREE GIFTS!

HARLEQUIN® *Blaze*®

red-hot reads!

YES! Please send me 2 FREE Harlequin® Blaze™ novels and my 2 FREE gifts (gifts are worth about $10). After receiving them, if I don't wish to receive any more books, I can return the shipping statement marked "cancel." If I don't cancel, I will receive 4 brand-new novels every month and be billed just $4.49 per book in the U.S. or $4.96 per book in Canada. That's a savings of at least 14% off the cover price. It's quite a bargain. Shipping and handling is just 50¢ per book in the U.S. and 75¢ per book in Canada.* I understand that accepting the 2 free books and gifts places me under no obligation to buy anything. I can always return a shipment and cancel at any time. Even if I never buy another book, the two free books and gifts are mine to keep forever.

150/350 HDN FV42

Name _____ (PLEASE PRINT) _____

Address _____ Apt. # _____

City _____ State/Prov. _____ Zip/Postal Code _____

Signature (if under 18, a parent or guardian must sign) _____

Mail to the **Harlequin® Reader Service:**
IN U.S.A.: P.O. Box 1867, Buffalo, NY 14240-1867
IN CANADA: P.O. Box 609, Fort Erie, Ontario L2A 5X3

Want to try two free books from another line?
Call 1-800-873-8635 or visit www.ReaderService.com.

* Terms and prices subject to change without notice. Prices do not include applicable taxes. Sales tax applicable in N.Y. Canadian residents will be charged applicable taxes. Offer not valid in Quebec. This offer is limited to one order per household. Not valid for current subscribers to Harlequin Blaze books. All orders subject to credit approval. Credit or debit balances in a customer's account(s) may be offset by any other outstanding balance owed by or to the customer. Please allow 4 to 6 weeks for delivery. Offer available while quantities last.

Your Privacy—The Harlequin® Reader Service is committed to protecting your privacy. Our Privacy Policy is available online at www.ReaderService.com or upon request from the Harlequin Reader Service.

We make a portion of our mailing list available to reputable third parties that offer products we believe may interest you. If you prefer that we not exchange your name with third parties, or if you wish to clarify or modify your communication preferences, please visit us at www.ReaderService.com/consumerchoice or write to us at Harlequin Reader Service Preference Service, P.O. Box 9062, Buffalo, NY 14269. Include your complete name and address.

HB13R

It was her. He knew it.

Eli Weston chuckled low, the sound rife with irony, then brought the bottle to his lips once again. Southern Comfort—appropriate, considering that was the only form of relief he was likely to get during this godforsaken week from hell. Water sloshed against the side of the tub and splashed onto the back porch as he deliberately shifted into a more relaxed position. It didn't matter that he was wound tighter than a two-dollar watch, that the mere thought of her sent a bolt of heat directly into his groin.

Perception, naturally, was key.

How did he know it was her who'd pulled into the driveway? The particular sound of her car door? The crunch of a light-footed person across the gravel? Those keen senses honed by years of specialized military training?

Ha. As if.

Nothing that sophisticated, unfortunately. It was the tightening of his gut, the prickling of his skin across the nape of his neck, the slight hesitation from the moment the car motor turned off until the driver decided to exit the vehicle. As though she was steeling herself, preparing to face him.

That was what had given her away.

"I'm back here," he called before she could mount the front porch steps.

She hesitated once again, then resumed movement and changed direction. Eli closed his eyes and prayed that she'd be in something other than that damned dress she'd had on earlier today. It was white, short and…flouncy. Not the least bit inappropriate, but somehow it managed to be sexy as hell all the same. It hugged her curvy frame, showcased her healthy tan and moved when she did. The hem fluttered just so with every swing of her hips, a silent "take me" with each step she took.

It was infuriatingly, unnervingly hot.

A startled "Oh" made him open his eyes, his gaze instinctively shifting toward the direction of the sound.

He mentally swore. Just his luck—she was still wearing it.

"There's a shower inside," she said tightly. "Could you get out of there? I need to talk to you."

He shrugged lazily, then stood. Water sloshed over the sides and sluiced down his body. He pushed his hair back from his face, careful to flex his biceps in the process.

He arched a deliberate brow. "Anything for you, sweetheart. Happy now?"

The last person Eli Weston can afford to be attracted to is the only woman he wants. Find out why by picking up THE RULE-BREAKER by Rhonda Nelson.

Available March 19.

A new installment in the bestselling Mighty Quinns series by Kate Hoffmann

When Jack Quinn's mother and Jenna McMahon's father hook up, the kids are not all right. But as Jenna and Jack work to keep their parents apart, they realize that family ties run deep, but passion and desire run even deeper.

Pick up

The Mighty Quinns: Jack

by *Kate Hoffmann*

AVAILABLE MARCH 19, 2013

Red-Hot Reads

www.Harlequin.com